LIVING FOR Love AND DYING FOR Loyalty 3

AN URBAN TALE OF LOVE BY MZ. LADY P

Main Menu

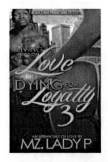

Start Reading

Acknowledgements

Copyright Notice

Table of Contents

Chapter 1-Rahmeek

As the bullets from Carmen's gun entered my mother's and sister's bodies, I immediately drifted off into space from being shocked at the events that were unfolding before my eyes. I was the reason for all of this. My thirst for money and power has put the crew and our families in danger. The sounds of the kids screaming and hollering jarred me from my deep thoughts.

"Call an ambulance now!" Momma Gail screamed as she applied pressure to my mother's wounds who was lying in a pool of blood on the floor unconscious. Boogie was on the floor holding Stacy who was bleeding profusely from a gunshot wound to her shoulder. She was alert but in a lot of pain.

"Nigga, this some straight bullshit! Rah, this shit is all your fucking fault! What the fuck were you thinking?" Boogie yelled as he applied pressure to Stacy's wound.

"I was thinking the same damn thing you were thinking! More ways to get this fucking bread!"

I started walking towards Boogie. He has been in his feelings ever since he found out that Hassan and I are Stacy's brothers. Before I could make it over towards him, Killa stepped in front of me.

"Kill all that shit right now! It is not the fucking time to be pointing fingers at one another! Let's find out where Markese, Nisa, and Hassan ran off to."

I never even realized they had exited the house. Killa and I ran out of the door trying to find out where they went. Gunshots in the distance made us haul ass down the long driveway. Nisa had Juan running with him on her hip and Markese had Gabriella on his shoulder running back towards the house. Hassan was shooting at Chico and the gunmen. He was laying

Chico's men down one by one. We all ran back towards the house and made it in safely. Sirens could be heard in the distance. I'm glad we have security cameras everywhere. The police would want to question everyone, but the tapes would tell the whole story. I didn't have time to be fucking with the police. I needed to make sure my people were straight.

"On every motherfucking thing I love, that bitch Carmen and that nigga Chico is dead!" Markese yelled as he checked Gabriella and Juan out.

"Man, Kese, I'm sorry. This shit is all my fault." I felt like I owed him that much.

"We all fucked up, Rah. Don't blame yourself for this shit. We were all bamboozled by that psychotic ass bitch," Markese said as he walked over to check on Trish. She was just coming to after being knocked out by Carmen.

The ambulance and the police had arrived. Boogie rushed out of the house carrying Stacy. Mike carried out my mother. They were placed into different ambulances and sped off. The police said that they would meet us at the hospital to ask questions. I handed them my lawyer's card. I'm not discussing this shit without my lawyer being present. Hassan, Killa, Nisa, and Markese followed the ambulances to the hospital. I had to check on the kids and the girls before I followed them.

"You cool, Trish?" I asked her because she was rubbing the back of her head. "I think you need to go to the hospital and get checked out."

"I'm good. I just want to stay here and make sure my babies are okay."

I ran up the stairs and found Niyah and Momma Gail in the nursery with the twins. Brooklyn, Lil Rahmeek, Lil Markese, Gabriella, and Juan were all still crying. I kissed all of them on their foreheads, thankful that they were not hit by any of the bullets.

"Ya'll okay?" I asked Niyah and Momma Gail.

"We're fine, Rahmeek. Go check on my daughter," Momma Gail said with a look of disappointment on her face. Niyah never even looked up at me. We were real close so I know she was real upset with me.

I walked into our bedroom and heard water running in the bathroom. I knocked on the door but there was no answer. I twisted the knob and went inside. Aja was on the floor in front of the toilet violently vomiting. I grabbed a towel and wet it. I placed it on the back of her neck as I rubbed her back. I was trying my best to make her feel better.

She roughly slapped my hand away from her. "Don't touch me Rahmeek!"

She stood up and gargled with mouthwash. She turned around and folded her arms. The look in her eyes let me know she was ready for an explanation.

"Baby, I'm so sorry. Everything I did was for us."

"Really? If that's the kind of gifts you're giving out these days, then you can keep it. One million dollars, huh? That's what you sold your dick for? Here I was thinking that our love is priceless. What does that make you, a male prostitute?"

My anger got the best of me and I started to choke her. Mainly, because her words were too disrespectful for me. I understood she was angry and hurt behind my actions but the words she was using were not called for.

"I know you're mad, Aja, but watch your mouth! I fucked up but I have no problem with fucking you up behind your jazzy ass mouth!" I let go of her throat and she started to cry.

"We have a family Rah. I'm pregnant with our second child and this is how you do me...do us? This is something I cannot forgive. This is the second time in a couple of months that you have stepped out on this marriage. I'm done. I think it's best that I take my baby and move out."

"You're not taking my son anywhere! We're in this shit until death do us part. I'm about to go to the hospital and check on my mother and sister. We'll finish talking about this when I get back."

I grabbed her by the chin and kissed her long and hard. She opened her mouth and invited my tongue in. She wrapped her arms around me tight and hugged me like I was going off to the joint to do a bid. I walked out of the house and went to the hospital.

Once I arrived, I was glad to know that my mother was going to make it. Stacy was going to be straight as well. I knew that I would have to explain my actions to the crew but that would have to wait. I needed to get home to my wife and make shit right with her. The only problem was that she and my son were gone when I made it to the crib. There was a letter on the bed. I sat down on the bed and began to read it. I wanted to cry but I was too gangster to let tears come from my eyes.

Dear Rahmeek,

I know that you're upset with me for leaving and taking the baby. You left me no choice. I have to find out if being with you is what I really want. After tonight, I'm not sure if I want us anymore. I love you with everything inside of me but I need to love Aja more. I cannot be stressed out with this pregnancy. Don't try and contact me. Let me figure this out for myself. If it's meant to be then we will be together. If not, thank you for the good times and our children. I will keep Markese and my parents informed of our whereabouts. Please don't spazz out and start murking people for no reason. Know that I love you with all my heart. I'm just trying to figure out if love is enough to keep this marriage going.

P.S Brooklyn is at Niyah and Hassan's house.

Love Always Aja

My ego was all fucked up. My wife walked out on me and took my seed. I want to find her and beat her ass but I know I brought this shit on myself. I'll just have to thug it out until she comes around. I still need to focus on my position with crew and being a better father to my children.

Chapter 2- Stacy

6 Months Later

My life has changed drastically in such a very short time. I still can't believe it. I went from having no family to having a husband, mother, and two brothers. I love having big brothers that are goons. Rahmeek and Hassan are the best. They smother and spoil me like I'm a toddler. Sometimes I hate it, but I must admit that it feels damn good. My mother, Ammenah, is the best. She is trying so hard to make up for all of the lost time. We have become so close these past couple of months. Since the shooting, she has had some health issues, but she will fully heal. Getting shot in the chest is no joke.

After I was released from the hospital, I was informed of the inheritance that Juan left for me. My check had been placed into an account for me. I am in possession of the funds he left me but Boogie refuses to let me touch it. He would rather us live off of his hard earned money.

I have never been to the house that Juan had built for me. Boogie is dead set against me going to see it. Rahmeek keeps asking me why I haven't been to look at the property. I just tell him I'll see it when I get a chance. I know he knows that Boogie is the reason why I won't go see it but he never comes out and says it.

I'm not going to put my brothers in my business, especially when it comes down to my husband. Boogie don't play about the crew being in our business. Lately, he has been so grumpy and distant. I just don't understand why he is not happy for me in regards to finding my brothers and mother. He makes sure he is not around whenever they come over.

Boogie is not fucking with Rahmeek period. He feels like the way shit has turned out for them is his fault. He is the only one still in his feelings about the shit besides Aja. The rest of us have moved on and trying to rebuild our broken family. The shit is getting old. Boogie is too damn young to be this fucking grumpy.

****

Today is his thirty-second birthday. I want to take him to the strip club but he told he doesn't celebrate his birthday. I don't care what he says I'm doing something nice for him anyway. He loves my cooking so I decided to cook him a candlelit dinner, lobster tails, T-bone steak, garlic bread, and Caesar salad.

I lit the candles all over the dining room. I had two bottles of Moet on chill and two Kush blunts already rolled and ready to be put in the air. A month ago, we were out shopping and we went inside a jewelry store. He had his eye on a diamond encrusted pinky ring with a matching chain. I made sure to go back and purchase it for him for his birthday. He deserves it. Plus, money ain't a thang. He spares no expense when it comes down to spoiling me. He has been car shopping, but was undecided on what he wanted. I noticed him eyeing a white on white Masarati. I had the dealership customize it to what I knew he would like. I also made sure to get him personalized plates that read "Boogie 1." I can't wait for him to see his gifts. He is going to be so happy.

I was rocking a red YSL bondage dress with a pair of snakeskin Red Bottoms. Trish had my hair and make-up on point. I sat at the dining room table waiting for him to arrive. Two hours later, I heard him pull into the driveway bumping *Blah, Blah, Blah* by Rich Homie Quan. I anticipated for him to walk through the door and see the happy look on his face. Unfortunately, the mean scowl on his face told me that happy was not what he was feeling at all.

"What the fuck is all of this Stacy? Oops, I mean Anastasia!"

I overlooked the fact that he called me by my real name. Lately, he has been doing that and its really starting to get under my damn skin.

"Happy Birthday, baby! Come over here and sit down to eat and open your gifts."

I walked towards him and wrapped my arms around his neck. He didn't even hug me back.

"What the fuck did I tell you? Didn't I say that I wasn't celebrating my birthday?"

"I know Boogie. I just wanted to do something special for my husband. Is there something wrong with that?"

"There's something wrong with the fact that your ass is hard headed and don't fucking listen to me."

Boogie walked away from me and went upstairs. I was done trying with this bi-polar ass nigga. I sat at the table and popped open the champagne bottle. I downed three glasses in a matter of minutes. Boogie still hadn't come back downstairs so I decided to go upstairs and get him so he could open up his gifts. They were too expensive for him not to at least open them.

I walked up the stairs slowly because I was hesitant about giving him the gifts. I was skeptical about his reaction to them. I entered our bedroom but he wasn't in there. I walked into our bathroom and my eyes were wide as hell. My husband was leaning over the sink snorting lines of coke off of a mirror. I was in utter shock and disbelief. I let out a gasp that made Boogie jump and knock the mirror off of the sink. I tried to walk away but he caught me before I was able to get away.

"Fuck is you doing spying on me now! What you going to do, run and tell everybody?"

Boogie had a crazy look in his eyes. All I could do was cry and attempt to get out of his grasp. He was still holding my arms tightly.

"I would never tell anybody your personal business. Please let me go. You're hurting me!"

He released my arm, walked back into the bathroom, and slammed the door. I went from upset to livid in a matter of seconds. I started to beat and kick on the door.

"Open this fucking door, Kendrick, right now! Is this why you have been acting all strange the last couple of months?" There was silence on the other end and that's when I heard him snorting that shit up his fucking nose.

"Happy Birthday, you fucking dope fiend!" I yelled and walked away from the bathroom door.

I didn't make it farther than the hallway. I never heard him come behind me. He spent me around towards him and slapped me so hard that I spun all the way around. I hit the wall and caused our wedding picture to fall to the floor and shatter. I was in such a daze I couldn't speak or cry.

"Watch your fuckin mouth! I'm not a damn dope fiend! You wanted to celebrate my birthday so get the fuck up! Let's celebrate!"

He yanked me up from the floor and wiped the blood from the corner of my mouth with his thumb.

"Go wash your face. We're going to the strip club like you wanted."

He walked down the stairs and I went into the bathroom. I washed my face and tried to fix my makeup. I was in shock. I never cried. Boogie has never cursed, raised his voice, or even hit me for that matter.

Him acting like a kid in the candy store let me know he had found his gifts. He was in the garage with the Masarati. I hurried downstairs and went into the garage. I put on a brave front but I was crumbling into a million pieces on the inside.

"Do you like it?" I asked in a cracked voice.

"Like it? Baby, I love it!"

Boogie rushed over to me and lifted me up of off the floor and kissed me passionately. He lifted me onto the hood of the car. He continued to kiss me roughly as he ripped my thong off of me. I was trying my best to hold back but his touch felt so good. I laid there and let him have his way with me. He pulled his shirt over his head and let his pants drop down to his ankles. Without hesitation, he rammed his dick into my awaiting wet pussy. All eleven inches of his dick were deep inside my pussy. He pounded inside and out of me. I tried to match thrust for thrust but I was no match for him.

Boogie's dick was harder than usual. It felt like a damn brick pounding inside of me. He was so rough with me. The shit was painful and pleasurable at the same time. I kept trying to grab him but he had my hands pinned up behind my head. He pulled out of me and flipped me over onto my stomach. He roughly grabbed my hair and inserted his dick back inside of me.

"I love you, Stacy. You know that right?" he said in between breaths and thrusts.

"Yeah, I know, Boogie."

"You feel good than a motherfucker. I'm about to bust all in this pussy!"

Seconds later, Boogie came but his ass was still hard as a rock. He had just literally beat the pussy up but he wasn't finished. He threw me over his shoulder and carried me into the house. We fucked in every room in all positions possible.

Once he was done, the sun was coming up. I laid under him and rested my head on his hairy chest. I couldn't wrap my mind around the fact that I had just saw three sides of my husband in a matter of hours. The fact that he was getting high had me all in my feelings. I wondered how long he had been snorting that shit. The crew has no idea about that shit. Markese would go ballistic if he knew Boogie was getting high. I looked up at his handsome sleeping face and I had no idea who he was. I couldn't believe I was sleeping with a stranger.

Chapter 3- Boogie

I'm feeling like shit right now. I can't believe I put my hands on Stacy. I love her to death and I would never want to hurt her. It's just that I have been so angry and agitated lately. The only thing that calms my nerves is heroin.

I have used occasionally but it has been on a regular basis these last six months. Heroin numbs all the pain and my past demons. No one knows of my drug use, but Stacy. Stacy is real loyal so I know she will never say anything to anyone else.

Since we stepped back from the game, I have been focused on my chain of barbershops. I have been trying to suppress memories of my fucked up childhood. My street life and focusing on getting money blocked my thoughts, but now it's been hard. I'm sitting on more bread than I know what to do with. I can retire for the rest of my life and my wife and I will be Gucci. Shit has changed drastically due to Rahmeek's greed. I know that I can't entirely blame him because we were all bamboozled by that psycho bitch Carmen. She better pray that I never catch her ass. I have a couple of bullets with her name written on them.

Ever since Stacy found out that Rahmeek and Hassan were her brothers and Ammenah was her mother, I barely get to spend any time with her. I need her at home with me. I know that I sound like a bitch right now, but besides the crew Stacy is all I have in regards to having a real family. My parents are dead and I'm an only child. As I sit here on the patio sipping on some Remy and smoking a blunt, I can't help but to think of my evil parents.

My mother beat me if I breathed the wrong way. I thought my name was motherfucker because that's all she ever called me. She hated me for existing. She would lock me inside closets for days at a time without food or water. I just knew that I would die in there. I would sit in the closet and wonder what I did to deserve all of this.

When I was seven, truant officers showed up to my house because I hadn't been to school in over a month. My mother was gone and I opened the door. I must have looked horrendous because I was removed from my mother's home. I went to live with my father. That shit was even worse than living with my mother. He turned out to be a raging alcoholic and a child molester. Every day that I lived with him was hell. He violated me in ways that no one should do to any human being, let alone their own child. He took care of the necessities I needed to survive but he was no father to me. When I was eleven, he ended up dying of cirrhosis of the liver.

The Department of Children and Family Services sent me to live with a foster family in the Roosevelt Towers. That's how I ended up meeting the crew. My foster mother never gave a fuck what we did as long as we were there when the social worker came. She made sure I was clothed and fed. The old bitch didn't have a loving bone in her body. All she wanted was a check.

Once I met Markese, it was on and popping. I hooked up with him and it's been fuck the world and get money ever since. The last time I heard anything about my mother, she had died of AIDS. I hope that bitch met the devil as soon as she breathed her last breath.

****

The only thing that I can think of is Stacy since I woke up this morning. I have got to get my shit together. I'm falling off and it's not a good look. I know Stacy is disappointed in me and that's the last thing I want for her to be. I have been thinking of ways to apologize to her. She was gone when I woke up this morning and she hasn't returned any of my calls.

I was happy as hell when I heard her car pull into the garage. I ran down the stairs to meet her at the door.

"Hey Baby. I've been calling you all day. Why didn't you answer your phone?"

"My phone is dead. I forgot to get the car charger."

I noticed that she never made eye contact with me as she looked inside the refrigerator.

"Come here. We really need to talk."

I grabbed her by the hand and led her into the living room. I sat down on the couch and pulled her onto my lap.

"I just want to say that I'm sorry about last night. I was way out of pocket for putting my hands on you. All you were trying to do was make my birthday special. You're too good of a wife for me to treat you with such disrespect."

"It's okay, Boogie." Stacy kept her head low. I grabbed her by the chin and looked into her eyes. I noticed that her bottom lip was a little swollen and that made me feel even worse.

"No, it's not okay. Putting that shit up my nose was not cool. It also wasn't cool for me to put my hands on you. I promise that, from this day forward, I'm done with that shit. I also apologize for not supporting you with finding out about your family. I guess I'm jealous because I don't have any family. All I have is you and now I have to share you with others. I'm not used to that at all. I'm glad you found them and going forward I will support you."

Stacy wiped the tears from her eyes and looked into mine. "I love you more than life itself. No matter who comes into my life, you will always come first. I'm sorry for not taking your feelings into consideration. I should have known it would bother you, due to your child hood. I will admit that it really hurt me to see you getting high. I'm telling you right now, if I ever find out you're still putting that shit your nose, I'm leaving and I mean it." The look on her face told me that she was dead ass serious.

"I promise, baby, I'm done with that shit."

I kissed her and she kissed me back. I slid my hand up her dress and I tried to put my hand in her panties, but she stopped me.

"Baby, I would love to have sex with you but my pussy is swollen from our session last night. My legs hurt so bad I'm going to need to soak in some hot water in order to get my shit back right."

"I was off that shit. I'm sorry if I was too rough."

"It was pleasurable. Your ass stayed on hard no matter how many times you came." We both laughed.

"I love you, Ma."

"I love you more. Now get dressed. we're going over to Niyah and Hassan's for a BBQ in honor of her brother coming home from the joint." Stacy rose up off of my lap and disappeared upstairs.

I forgot all about Marlo. His ass did five years straight in the joint. That nigga was all about getting that money but he was a hot head and bad for business. He was getting money with us but Markese had to cut him loose due to all the heat he was bringing to the Towers. Shortly after, he was booked for drug and gun Possession. I hope he gets out and chill. We are all out of the game and living good. The last thing we need is to murk his ass for bringing heat or getting out of pocket. That nigga was always plotting and up to no good.

Chapter 4-Niyah

Raising twins has got to be the hardest shit ever. Hassan Jr. and Hadiyah are seven months old and getting big as ever. It's a struggle trying to keep up with their asses and Hassan is no fucking help. He's more focused on opening up the club. He, Rahmeek, and Markese are getting ready for the grand opening of their strip club, "Gentleman's Paradise." At first, I was skeptical. I put up a good fight and argument, but in the end, Hassan won the battle. I have to trust that my husband will not give into temptation. He has never given me a reason to question his loyalty so I wasn't about to start questioning it now. If he knows what's good for him, he will keep his dick in his pants. I'm not Aja and Trish. All that damn cheating shit is not flying with me. I'm going to jail and I mean that shit.

It's hard to believe that it's been five years since my older brother Marlo has been gone. I swear I have missed him so much. I can't wait for the twins to meet their uncle. I also can't wait for him to meet Hassan. I hope and pray that Lo is on his best behavior. Before he got locked up, he was in the streets wilding and living reckless. He constantly kept putting all of our lives in danger. At first, he was mad at Markese for cutting him off, but after some years behind bars, he put his ill feelings towards Markese behind him.

Lately, he has been asking about Aja. I just keep telling him that she is married and to leave her alone. He doesn't care about that shit. Aja was the only person he ever cared about. Aja was his everything. He took her virginity and laid claim to her. She was so in love with him but he started cheating and running the streets so she ended up leaving him. Marlo needs to understand that she is married to my husband's brother. The last thing I need is beef within the family. We all just got back on track since that Carmen bullshit.

I'm glad to have Ammenah in our lives. She is the best mother in law and grandmother a girl could ever have. Stacy is a big help as well. She keeps the kids all the time just to give me a break. Hassan has been so happy since he found his mother. It's like he smiles more and his eyes glisten with just the mention of her name. I just wish that he would spend more time with his family, but I know he is going hard to provide us a better life.

Hassan is the best husband a girl could ever ask for. When we first met, we were on just some fucking type of shit. Who would have known that we would be happily married with children? I thank God for him each and every day. Truth be told, he saved me from the streets. Before I met him, I was out here fucking with a different dude every other week just to keep my pockets fat and my attire accurate. I didn't fuck for shoes or no damn Rainbow outfits. If I was fucking, a nigga he was lacing me with nothing but the best. I have to admit Hassan introduced me to the lavish lifestyle.

My mother gave up on me and Marlo a long time ago. She was a devout Christian woman and she didn't condone the way we were living our lives. She put us out of her house and moved to Meridian, Mississippi. We talk on a regular and she sends the kids clothes. I would love for my mother to come to my house for a visit, but she refuses to step a foot inside of my door due to Hassan's lifestyle. That's fine with me. she can stay her self-righteous ass in the damn country. I don't need her judgmental ass disrespecting my husband. It's because of him that I'm happy and living well. No one will look down on him or belittle him for his line of work, not even the person who birthed me.

****

As I pulled up to the Greyhound bus terminal, I noticed Marlo. He was dressed in jailbird attire, white t-shirt, and gray jogging pants. I'm glad he was rocking the white Air Forces I sent him last month. He was cocky as hell and had gotten a little taller. His once short hair was now in long braids. We had to get that shit cut immediately. Don't nobody wear braids anymore.

"What's up, lil sis? Damn I missed you," Marlo said as he pulled me into his arms and hugged me tightly.

"I missed you too, Lo. Let's go home so you can take that shit off. I have you a whole new wardrobe at the house."

"Thanks again for letting me stay at your spot until I get on my feet. I plan on doing that ASAP."

"I hope you're not thinking about getting back out here in these streets. A lot of shit has changed out here since you've been gone. Niggas getting murked every day." A feeling of dread came over me because I knew how he got down in the streets.

"I'm good, sis. I got some shit lined up. It's legit so don't worry."

How the fuck could he tell me not to worry? I know his ass is up to no good. He hasn't been out of jail twenty-four hours and he's on bullshit. He better hope I don't find out. The last thing I need is drama where I lay my head. Pulling up to the house, I could tell that Marlo was in awe of it. His eyes were as big as saucers as we made our way up the winding driveway.

"Damn! Your ass living like the rich and famous. Dude got long money if y'all living like this."

I watched Marlo as the wheels in his head started to turn. He always loved materialistic shit and never cared how he got it. All I could do was hope and pray that he stayed on the straight and narrow.

****

The BBQ was in full swing and everyone had arrived except for Aja. It was good to see the crew back together after all of the bullshit that transpired. I was even more surprised to see Boogie in attendance. He hasn't been kicking it at all. It was good to see him and Rahmeek talking. At one point, I thought they were going to have a gunfight.

The spades table and the dominoes table were going on. I hate when these niggas play shit like this because all they do is argue.

"Domino, motherfucker!" Rahmeek yelled to Markese as he downed a shot of Remy. I noticed he had been knocking shots back but that ain't none of my business.

Finally, my brother came outside and joined us. He was rocking a white and gold Hudson shirt with white shorts to match along with a fresh pair of high top Air Force Ones.

"Damn! You clean up real nice," I said as I hugged him.

I went around the tables and introduced him to the people who were there that he didn't know. I could tell that seeing Markese for the first time had him a little on edge, but he remained cordial. Finally, Aja arrived. I was so happy to see her. It's been a minute since she has been around.

"It's about time! I missed you so much." I hugged her tightly. We walked over to the bar, grabbed a drink and joined Stacy, Trish, and Nisa by the pool. I watched as Rahmeek and Marlo watched her like a hawk. She looked past Rahmeek as if he wasn't there.

"I know that ain't my baby, Aja."

Marlo picked her up and kissed her on the mouth. The look on everyone's face said it's about to be some shit and I prayed I wouldn't be in the middle of it.

Chapter 5- Aja

I have had a lot of time on my hands to think about my marriage. I really don't know if I still want to be married. I love Rahmeek with all of my heart, but how much can my heart take? Love is not supposed to hurt and I am really hurt behind Rahmeek's betrayal. My heart is too broken to be repaired right now. Ever since I left him, I have had peace of mind and there is nothing like that. Don't get me wrong, I miss his touch, kiss, and that dick is what I miss the most. I just can't deal with the fact that he sold his himself. He said fuck love and greed took over. We all know where being greedy got his stupid ass.

A week after I left my home, I suffered a miscarriage. I was so hurt behind his actions that I cried all day every day. the fetus couldn't take the stress. I wasn't really ready for a baby anyway. As far as our relationship goes, we really don't have a personal one. Our conversations are strictly about Lil Rah and Brooklyn. Since Karima is still in jail and Rahmeek is busy trying to open up his club, I decided to let Brooklyn stay with me during the week and Rah on the weekends. Since the shooting, Ammenah has moved into our house to help out with the kids. She has been a really big help to us. At first Rahmeek tried his best to get me to come back to him , but I wasn't trying to hear all that sweet talking shit. After while, he just gave up. Now he is in his fucking feelings. We don't talk or see each other. Our interactions are strictly through Ammenah and I don't give a fuck. He has a lot of nerve walking around with his ass on his shoulders. He's the reason why all this shit is going on anyway. Lord knows I love my husband, but I'm not for any of his bullshit these days.

I wasn't really feeling coming to the BBQ. I wasn't ready to face my husband or my first love. I knew it would be awkward. As soon as I walked into the backyard, I locked eyes with my husband. I hurried up and turned my head. He is just too fucking fine. No matter what the occasion is, Rah stays on point. His dreads are always freshly twisted and his attire is always very accurate. I stared at him longer than I should have because he was trying his best not to look at me, but I know he peeped my sexy ass. It's been years since I laid eyes on Marlo. Jail had done that niggas body good. I watched as he walked towards me like he owned the world. He still had the cutest light-skinned baby face that I fell in love with. I was caught off guard when Marlo kissed me. I forgot Rahmeek was even there. His lips were soft as hell. I kissed him back and the shit felt good. For a moment, I was lost in his kiss and flashbacks of the way we used to be flashed in my mind. I was immediately jolted back into reality when I felt myself get yanked by the back of my neck and pushed into the house.

"Bitch, I know you have lost your mind kissing on another nigga in my face." Rahmeek had pushed me up against the sink with his hands around my throat.

"He kissed me, Rah. It's not my fault!"

"Fuck outta here. You kissed that nigga back. We all saw your trifling ass!" I managed to pry his hands from around my neck.

"Nigga, you have a lot of nerve! Not too long ago, you stepped out on your marriage. That's why we're separated now with your dick selling ass."

I never saw the smack coming and neither did he because I slapped his ass right back and we started rumbling all over that kitchen. I was throwing glasses and anything else I could find. He kept smacking and choking me, but I wasn't giving up without a fight. I was making sure I left some war wounds on his ass. I punched his ass in his eye. I prayed that I blacked his shit. Not long after, everyone came in and tried to break us apart. Finally, they were able to separate us and the looks in their faces was nothing, but disappointment in both of us. I couldn't believe what we had become. I was so embarrassed.

"Rahmeek and Aja, this shit is unacceptable. I can't believe y'all disrespecting Niyah and Hassan like this. I have watched your behavior these last couple of months and it is sickening. Don't y'all know them babies are hurting because they are stuck in the middle of this chaos?" Ameenah stood in the middle of the kitchen with her hands on her hips. "Marriage is not easy. That's why it takes two to make it work, but from the looks of it, you hate each other. Either ya'll going to be together or you're not. If you're not, then sign the papers and be done with the shit. I think I can speak for everyone when I say we are tired of this drama. No matter what is going on, we have to have an episode of the Rahmeek and Aja show. My blood pressure is through the fucking roof!"

"I'm sorry Ma. I-."

"Shut up, Rahmeek! I can't believe you put your hands on her like that." Ammenah pushed her way past everyone and went back outside.

"So, what's it going to be, Aja? You walked out on me. I've been trying to fix it, but obviously, you're showing me that you're done. If it's over, keep it one hundred and I will leave you alone."

Rahmeek stood there with pleading eyes, but he spoke the words in a harsh tone. I thought long and hard. I guess I took too long to answer his question.

"You know what, your silence speaks volumes. I get the picture. Don't worry Aja, I'm going to make sure my son is straight."

Rahmeek jerked away from Hassan and Markese. I observed Marlo standing in the doorway with a smirk on his face.

"That hoe is all yours," Rahmeek said to Marlo as he walked out of the door. He cranked up his motorcycle and drove off.

"I'm sorry ya'll, but the BBQ is over. Marlo, bring your ass in here right now!" Niyah said pissed off.

I looked at my brother's face and I knew he was mad at me. Everyone was mad at me. Tears welled up in my eyes and I ran to the bathroom and cried like a baby. I love Rahmeek; I really do. It's not fair that he gets to cheat on me and life is supposed to go back to normal. I stayed in that bathroom for an hour. Once I gathered myself, I walked out in the backyard and everyone was gone. I was getting ready to leave, but Marlo stopped me before I could leave.

"I'm sorry about that. It's just that I haven't seen you in so long. It reminded me of how in love we were."

"It's cool, Lo. I'm glad you're here, but I really needed to get home and pick up my son." I tried to walk past him but he grabbed me. He pecked me on the cheek.

"Stop crying. You know I hate it when you cry. Please don't leave. Finish celebrating with me. Everyone else is gone."

I should have left because, two blunts and a fifth of Remy later, Marlo had me spread-eagled, fucking the shit out of me. He took all his frustration out on my pussy. That shit felt good. It had been six months since I had some dick and I was sexually frustrated. The next morning I woke up to a banging headache and Niyah standing over us.

"Hurry up and get your ass out of that bed before Hassan catches you," Niyah said just above a whisper.

"Too late, Niyah. Let me holla at you real quick."

Hassan looked at me with disgust and I looked down in shame. Marlo was sleeping like a baby. I wanted to reach over and slap fire from his ass. How could he sleep through this shit?

"Please Hassan! Don't tell Rah on me."

"Aja, get your ass out of that bed and go get my fucking nephew! I love you sis, but you're dead ass wrong. I never took you for being the ratchet type."

Hassan left the room and snatched Niyah with so much force. I could actually hear them arguing and tussling. Hassan had really hurt my feelings. I was far from ratchet. In my heart, I knew that Hassan didn't mean what he said. He was just mad at me for what I did. In twenty-four hours, my marriage ended, I fucked Marlo and liked it. Fuck my life. I walked out of the house and prayed Hassan didn't tell Rah on my thot ass.

Chapter 6- Rahmeek

For as long as I live, Aja will always be number one in my life. However, I can't deal with her blatant disrespect for me and herself. I know that I should be the last one to talk about respect. I take ownership of my fuck-ups. Aja doesn't. Kissing that nigga in front of everyone has me wanting to put a bullet in her head. That nigga knew exactly what he was doing. I saw the smirk on his face as I walked out of the house. I love Niyah with all my heart, but her brother is a dead man if he thinks that he will ever disrespect me again and live to tell about it.

Despite stepping back from the drug game, I'm still the same nigga that shoots first and ask no questions. I don't give a fuck what Aja says; she is my wife and will be until the day I die. I know that she is mad at me, but it's been six months since that Carmen fiasco. How fucking long is she going to walk around mad at me? I miss being at the crib with my wife and kids. I wonder if she is really done. Despite her hesitation to answer my question, Aja's eyes tell her soul. I know that she still loves me; I just hurt her too much. I really appreciate her taking Brooklyn in. Lord knows I needed the help. The club has been taking up all of my time. We only have one week until the grand opening. Hassan, Markese, and I have invested so much fucking money into this club everything has to be on point. Everything is in place all we have to do is open. We're about to take the Chicago nightlife by storm.

****

It's my weekend with the kids and Aja should be here any minute. Since we pissed my mother off, she refuses to do our talking for us. I was taking out the garbage when I saw her car pulled up to the front of the house. I watched as she got out wearing some tight ass pants that made my dick get hard instantly. I couldn't help but look at her ass. *Why she got to be so fucking sexy?* I thought to myself. Aja is beautiful inside and out. My actions turned her ugly. I slowly walked up to greet her and the kids. As I approached the car, I noticed her trying not to look at me or pay me any attention. My dick was getting harder just looking at her.

Lil Rah reached his hands up for me to get him out of the car seat.

"Calm down, Lil Rah. I'll get you out in a damn minute." Aja said in frustration as she spoke Brooklyn started to get agitated in her car seat and started to whine and reach for me as well.

"Y'all can stop all that damn crying. Before we got here, you were cool." She started to unbuckle the straps on their car seats.

"Why the fuck are you cursing at them like that?"

"Shut up talking to me."

"You shut the fuck up and stop talking to them like that. I know you're mad at me, but don't take it out on my motherfucking kids."

I reached inside and grabbed Lil Rah and she grabbed Brooklyn. We both walked to the front door, Aja was behind me. Once we got inside I sat Lil Rah on the couch and turned around to grab Brooklyn. That's when I noticed Aja had tears falling from my eyes.

"What the fuck you crying for?" Aja tried to hurry up and run out the door, but I ran after her.

"Please, Rahmeek, let me go! I have to get out of here." She was squirming and fighting trying to get away from me.

"If you're crying because of me, all I can say is that I'm sorry for everything I've put you through." I've seen Aja cry before, but these tears were different. This shit was hurting me because no matter what, this shit is my fault.

"It's not fair. This is not supposed to be our life. I can't believe these kids are living house to fucking house because we can't get our shit together. What happened to us, Rahmeek? I'm so mad that I'm taking my frustration out on the kids. Look at us; we can't even be in the same room without arguing or fighting."

"Baby, I don't want to fight anymore. Please stay here and let me make it up to you. I can't sleep at night because you're not beside me." I pulled Aja into my embrace and held on to her tightly.

"I don't want to fight either, but I can't be with you if you're going to keep cheating on me. That shit is so embarrassing. I'm tired of all this madness going on in my marriage. All I want is to grow old with you and have a prosperous life. I have to know that I'm all you need and want. If I'm not enough for you, let's sign the papers and be done with this shit."

"You're all I want and need, Aja. Just give me a chance, Ma. I need my family back." I leaned in and kissed Aja and she grabbed my face and kissed me long and hard.

"I love you so much, Rah." Aja said in between kisses.

"I love you too."

"Thank God, ya'll made up. Give me my grandkids. I'll take them over to my house with me. Both of you need some alone time with each other." We both looked up at my mother and laughed.

The tension between us was still thick after my mother left with the kids. Aja was still sitting on the couch scrolling through her phone. I grabbed a bottle of Remy from the fridge and poured both of us a drink.

"You want to go out and grab something to eat?" I handed her the drink and sat next to her on the couch.

"Yeah. I'm down with that. Where are you taking me?"

"I was thinking we could go to the club and have the chef hook us up some dinner."

"The club isn't open yet. How are you going to do that?"

"I'm the boss." I kissed her on the cheek and we headed out of the door.

I called the chef into the club and told him what I wanted him to make for Aja. In the meantime, I showed her around the club. I could tell she wasn't feeling the stripper floor, but I tried my best to assure her she had nothing to worry about.

"I'm so proud of ya'll. This club is going to be off the chain. I think I need to come and show these niggas my skills on that pole." Aja did a little twerk as she swung around the pole.

"Don't get fucked up."

I pulled her close to me and lifted her onto the office in my desk. Our tongues danced and I pulled down her pants. I was glad she didn't have on any panties underneath. Her neatly shaved pussy looked delicious to me. I had to get a taste of her sweet nectar. I pushed her back on the desk and dived in tongue first. I took my time licking each and every inch of her pussy. I inserted my entire tongue in her pussy and began to make love to her with it.

Aja came in my mouth. I immediately turned her around and bent her over the desk. I dropped my pants and my boxers and entered her without hesitation. I pounded her pussy with no mercy. I was all up in her guts, damn near touching her soul.

"Aaaargh!" Damn Rahmeek! I watched as Aja grabbed the sides of the desk.

"You fucked that nigga, huh?" I pounded in and out of harder and smacked her ass at the same time. I was about to punish her for giving that nigga something that belongs to me.

"What?" she asked sounding dumbfounded. I knew that she was fully aware of what I had just said.

"Yeah, I heard you fucked that nigga." I grabbed her hair and wrapped it around my hands. I wanted her to feel some pain and the pleasure. I brought my face down close to her so that my mouth was close to her ear.

"Make that your last fucking time. Let me find out y'all on some bullshit. Both of y'all gone feel my heat."

I continued to fuck her until I let all my seeds loose inside of her. Once we were finished, we got dressed in silence. I could tell she was scared to look at me.

"I know you think I'm mad about you fucking dude, but I'm not. I have no right to be. We weren't together. We're even. I don't want to hear anything about him or any other nigga."

"I better not find out you fucking no bitches either. I'm whooping her ass and I'm going to shoot the shit out of you. So, don't fuck with me, Rahmeek."

I looked in her eyes and saw how serious she was. Aja had nothing to worry about. I was done fucking other bitches. That shit was nothing but a fucking headache.

I knew that we were going to be fine. I could trust her. On the other hand, I knew I had to watch that nigga Marlo like a hawk. I had a strong feeling he was going to make me dust off my Desert Eagles.

Chapter 7- Trish

Lord knows I love Markese, but I think this nigga builds me up to bring me down. This nigga had me thinking that he had a change of heart about our son's paternity when all along he had swabbed his mouth. He is so damn smart that he's dumb. Why would he use our address on the application? He received a letter in the mail informing him that their office had been broken into and his test was one of the files that were stolen, but we have nothing to worry about.

I should have known better than to believe that he went from being doubtful to a hundred percent sure in a matter of hours. I have been the best wife that I could be to him, but I don't know how much more I can deal with. It hurts me to my heart to even think he was that doubtful that he would swab our son's mouth. I don't give a fuck if Gabriella and Juan do look like him. I bet his ass didn't swab their mouths and that shit hurts me even more. I love Markese so much. I love that nigga more than I love myself. That's a problem. I've been giving Markese all of me since I was fourteen and right now I'm feeling like love isn't enough to keep me in this marriage. The lies and deceit are too much for me.

I just killed a pint of Remy. He better hope I've calmed down before he makes it in this house. I made sure to call Aja and Momma Gail and tell them what he did. I made them promise not to say anything. I wanted to curse his ass out first. Since my kidnapping, I have been having nightmares about being raped by that psycho Mont. I'm glad I know his bitch ass is definitely dead this time. Now all I have to do is kill Carmen. I still have a knot in the back of my head from that bitch hitting me with that gun.

Besides finding out about Markese's latest act of disloyalty, we have been doing good. My shop is constantly expanding. Markese is opening the club soon. The kids are getting big and are healthy. People on the outside would swear we had the picture perfect life. At times, I believe we do have the picture perfect life, but then he pulls a stunt like this. I'm sick and fucking tired of putting on a show with his lying ass.

About an hour later, he pulled into the driveway and I couldn't wait for him to walk in the door.

"I'm going to ask you this once and one time only. If you lie, I'm knocking the shit out of you." I said as I got up in his face.

"What the fuck is wrong with you?"

"Did you have a paternity test done on Lil Markese?"

"Man, hell naw, you tripping, Trish." I knew his ass was lying so I punched his ass right in the mouth and his shit started to bleed.

"You lying motherfucker!" I threw the papers at his ass. I watched as he stood there and read them. He was cold busted and he knew it.

"I'm sorry. I just had to know."

"I understand that, Markese, but why would you do it behind my back. That shit was so foul."

I walked over to him and mushed his ass upside the head.

"I know you're mad, but you better not put your fucking hands on me again."

We were in each other's face staring one another down.

"Or what? You gon' beat the shit out me? You might as well get ready because we gon' rumble in this bitch."

"Let me get the fuck out of here."

He grabbed his car keys and tried to walk out of the door. I stood in his way and blocked him from leaving.

"Your ass ain't going nowhere. I'm not done talking about this shit."

"The shit is over and done with. I'm done talking. Now get the fuck out my way."

He tried to lift me up and move me. I went crazy and just started swinging on his ass like a mad woman. He slapped me so fucking hard that I flew over the damn couch. He tore the papers up and walked out of the house. I just laid on the floor I didn't even have it in me to cry anymore. I was officially tired of his ass. I got off of the floor and went upstairs to fix myself up. My face was red and swollen. The kids were with Gail so, I decided to go out to the bar and have a drink. That slap wasn't about to faze me. All I do is work and sit in this fucking house with these damn kids. I need to go out and kick it and see what's to this nightlife. The nights of me being home alone and crying myself to sleep are fucking over.

****

I decided to go to Lalo's since it was a bar and grill. I was hungry as hell, plus the margaritas will have a bitch on the moon. Since it was a Saturday night, I knew that it was about to be jumping because they played house music. It's always packed on the weekends. I ordered the steak taco platter and a strawberry margarita. I made sure to tell the waitress to keep the margaritas coming. Once I ate my food and drunk my first margarita I had to go to the washroom. As I got up from my seat, I bumped into the finest Puerto Rican *papi* I had ever seen.

"I'm sorry beautiful."

"It's cool. It actually was my fault."

I couldn't help, but to take in his features. He had thick black hair that was braided in two braids down his back. His face looked smooth. His lips were so damn pink and juicy. His attire was casual and real classy. He carried himself with so much confidence. I had to hurry up and walk past him. I was tipsy and the way my pussy was feeling right now, he could definitely get it tonight. I proceeded to the bathroom and handled my business. Once I exited, he was standing outside the door.

"Are you stalking me?"

"Actually I am. I didn't get your name and number?"

"That's because I wasn't giving it. As you can see, I'm married." I lifted my finger up and flashed my rock at his ass.

"Where'd your nigga get that from, a Cracker Jack box?"

"You tried it." I couldn't believe this nigga was trying to talk about my ring.

"I'm just fucking with you, Ma. You're a beautiful black woman and I would love to spend some time with you." He held my hand the entire time he was talking to me.

"I'm sorry, but I don't cheat on my husband."

"I'm not asking you to cheat on your husband. I'm asking for your name and number. Anything beyond that will be your call."

This nigga was talking real slick and I was loving it. His thick Puerto Rican accent was sexy as hell. He stroked the side of my face as he spoke to me.

"What's your name beautiful? I'm Yasir."

"I'm Trish. Nice to meet you, Yasir."

"So, what up with that number?"

"How about you give me your number and I'll call you when I get a chance."

"Deal but don't have me waiting long."

Yasir took my phone out of my hand and entered his number. I watched him as he walked back to where his friends were. I went back to my table and drank another margarita. I was wasted and it was time for me to head home. Yasir eye balled fucked me all night and if I didn't leave soon, I was going to be calling that nigga *papi* by morning.

Chapter 8-Carmen

My life has been on a downward spiral since that bitch Trish found out about my kids. Gabriella and Juan were a secret for so long. Back then, I wanted her to find out so bad. Now I wish she never found out about us. All I want is my family back.

Life was so much easier when I had my kids, my father, and Markese. My biggest regret was killing my father. All he ever did was love me and give me the world. In return, I blamed him for my weaknesses I had for a nigga. I wish I could take it all back. When I was lying in that casket, there were two things running through my head. I repented over and over again for my sins. If I made it out alive, I thought about the many ways that I would kill Trish.

I had my strategy all planned all out. Unfortunately, my mother, Lupe Rodriquez, had other plans. Once she heard of Juan's death, she put me under surveillance. I never knew that she had her right hand man Chico following me. Thank God he was. As soon as Chico and his men retrieved me from the grave, I was taken to Mexico. It had been years since I had seen my mother. Lupe was all I had left.

The plane ride was long as hell. I couldn't wait to make it to my mother's house. I wanted to hug her and tell her how much I missed her. However, that was not what I would be able do. As I walked through the door of her compound, I looked around at all of the massive structures. The ceilings were high and had a mural of her on the wall. I looked around and noticed armed men everywhere. I stood in the foyer scared to move. Minutes later, Lupe emerged looking like the drug czar she was. She walked right past me and into the sitting room. She sat down and gestured for me to sit next to her. I sat across from her. There was something about her cold stare and her demeanor that frightened me.

"As I sit here and look at you all I can see is disappointment." I could barely understand her because of her Spanish accent.

"Mother, I'm not sure I understand what you're talking about."

"You are your father's child. You're weak just like him. I can't believe you let a common thug destroy your life and everything you have worked for." She stood up from the couch and she poured a shot of tequila.

"I can't help the fact that I loved Markese. Let's not forget you ruined your family just like I did-over a man."

Lupe walked towards me and slapped me across the face with so much force that I thought my jaw shifted.

"I am Lupe Rodriquez. Don't you ever disrespect me. Daughter or no daughter, I will put a bullet in your head. From this point on, we do things my way. For starters, you need to go see my plastic surgeon. It's time you pay the people who wronged us a surprise visit."

Lupe kissed me on the cheek and walked away. I felt like she'd given me the kiss of death. It was her idea to change my identity and trick their asses. I only wanted revenge against Trish and Markese because I wanted my babies back. All I wanted was my mother's love. I thought that if I carried out her plan things would work out between us. Markese was able to get the kids from us and Ammenah and Anastasia survived.

Lupe was disappointed in me and Chico. She ordered him back to Mexico. I was not allowed to come back. I had to stay in Chicago and fix my mess. At that point, I realized that Lupe didn't care about me or my kids. Since the incident, I have been taking a chance by staying at the house Markese brought for me. I know that this is the last place he would ever come. I keep looking through all of our family photos when shit was good. A person on the outside would think that we were a big happy family. He was with us on holidays, birthdays, and all other special occasions. I'm trying to wrap my mind around the fact that Trish could ever think she was the main bitch. She was the real side bitch and she never even realized it.

Patron has become my best friend these days. I wake up drinking and I go to sleep drinking. It's my way of coping with this shitty thing called my life. I hardly ever leave the house but tonight I feel like seeing some fireworks. I jumped inside my Mercedes Benz truck and drove to the gas station. I filled up two gas cans with gasoline. I drove another hour towards my destination. It was two in the morning so I knew the place was empty. I exited my car carrying the gasoline cans. I walked to the back of the establishment and found the alarm system. I cut the wires that would alert the police that there was a break-in. The back door was made of glass. I looked around on the ground for something to throw through the glass. I finally found a brick and tossed it through the window causing it to shatter. I stepped through the door and I began to pour gasoline everywhere. I made sure to put some in the office area and reception area. Once I was done putting down the gasoline, I exited the door I came in. I pulled a box of Newport's from my pocket and retrieved a cigarette. I lit it with a match. I threw the match back into the establishment. I smoked my cigarette and watched as the entire place became engulfed in flames. It looked like the Fourth of July as the flames took over the sky. It was such a beautiful sight to me. I would love to see Trish's face when she sees her shop burned down to the ground. She took everything from me that I love. It's only right that I return the favor.

As I drove back home, the wheels in my head started to turn. The only thing I'm worried about is getting my kids back. I'm not going to lurk in the shadows and fuck them up. I'm about to do it in their motherfucking faces and there is nothing they will be able to do about it.

The next morning I woke up bright eyes and bushy tailed. I took a shower and got dressed in a beautiful white maxi dress with a pair of Michael Kors thong sandals. It's the first day of summer and the weather is beautiful.

Once I was finished with my hair. I was ready to hit the twelfth district police station. It was imperative that I get in contact with the Missing Persons Unit. Especially, since they think I'm dead and it's obvious that I'm alive and kicking. I walked into the police station looking like a million dollars.

"Hello. I need to speak to someone in regards to a missing person's case."

The woman officer looked up at me and rolled her eyes. "Who is missing, ma'am?"

"I am."

I had the officer's full attention now. She picked up the phone and made a call. After a couple more minutes, a plain clothes officer approached me and escorted me into a private office. I don't do white men but this officer had swag. He was rocking an all black t-shirt with a pair of black Levis along with a pair of black Timberland boots. His hair was black and short with a greasy look to it. I looked down at his crotch area and he was packing. His manhood as sitting on his thigh. I was straight eyeball fucking the man.

"I'm Detective Carmine Rizzo and I will be taking your report. I was told that you were the missing person. I'm actually confused. usually a family member comes in to report's a loved one missing. So, excuse me but this is a first for me."

He sat across from me and waited for me to respond. *It's now or never Carmen. The sooner you tell him, the quicker your babies will be back with you.*

"I'm Carmen Rodriquez and I have been missing for over a year. I was in Mexico because I feared for my life. I actually looked different back then but I needed plastic surgery to change my identity."

"If you don't mind me asking, who are you afraid of?"

"My children's father, Markese Jackson. He is a well known drug dealer and murderer."

"If you really fear for your life, why would you return after all this time?"

"I want my children and he is holding them hostage. His wife has turned them against me. He told me that he was going to kill me if I tried to get my kids back. Not to mention, I was the star witness in the murder of my father Juan Rodriquez."

I had his full attention now. He was eating this shit up. He walked out of the room and brought in some more officers. I told them the same story with more detail. The officer told me that due to me missing and the lack of evidence the murder charges were dropped but could be picked back up with concrete evidence linking Markese and Rahmeek to the murder. I prayed they didn't start asking questions about the murder. I forgot all about that. That's because I try my best to forget the fact that I am the one who really murked my father. The only thing I wanted was my kids.

To my surprise, Detective Rizzo was able to get paperwork from Child Protective Services. I am their legal guardian. Markese has no rights to my children, especially since he never even signed the birth certificates. I remember begging him to sign them but he was too worried about Trish finding out. I'm glad his ass didn't sign. A judge drew up the necessary documents that were needed to get the kids removed from their home and back with me. I accompanied the police to their address. I was getting my kids by any means necessary. I'm about to have one up on their asses. I made sure to tell the police I wanted twenty-four hour protection because I know this nigga will not stop until I'm dead.

Chapter 9- Markese

"Baby, please stop crying. I promise that I will have you another shop built from the ground up."

I tried my best to confront Trish but nothing was helping. Seeing her standing in the spot where her shop used to be is killing me slowly. I pulled her into my embrace and wrapped my arms around her.

"I don't want another shop. I have put my blood, sweat, and tears into this shop. Somebody did this shit on purpose. This shit got your psychotic ass baby momma's name written all over it. If you had kept your dick in your pants, my shop wouldn't be burnt to a fucking crisp. I swear I want to kill this bitch with my bare hands."

"If you would have done the shit right the first time then we wouldn't be going through this shit now, would we?"

As soon as the words left my mouth, I regretted it but Trish was foul for the shit she had said. I was just angry that she even brought up the bitch's name because I knew the bitch did the shit. No one in the city of Chicago had the heart to fuck with my wife besides her. Trish yanked away from me and got into the car. I talked to the Fire Marshall and found out that the fire was started with an accelerant and that's what made it burn so quickly. Since it was arson, there would have to be an investigation to make sure Trish didn't purposely start the fire in order to receive the insurance money. She was even more livid when I told her that.

The drive home was silent. I wasn't even about to strike up a conversation with Trish. I had a lot going on in my life right now. I couldn't deal with her taking her anger out on me, no matter if it was somewhat my fault.

The club opens up in a week and we are putting together the final details. We have hired nothing but the baddest bitches from all around to work at the club. I hired the best stripper out of the ATL named Yoshi Love to come and work for us. She would also be in charge of all the girls so she had to have her shit on point. We are putting her up in her own condo and giving her a company car. Her ass better be worth it or she will be on the midnight train to Georgia.

I pulled into our driveway and police cars pulled in behind me. I immediately jumped out of the car and Trish followed.

"What the fuck is going on, Officer and why are you on my property?" I was heated as soon as I saw Carmen exit another patrol car with a plain-clothes officer.

"Oh hell no! I'm about to whoop this bitch's ass!" Trish charged towards Carmen but was quickly placed in handcuffs. She was fighting and kicking the officer and everything. That only made him get rough with her.

"Get your hands off my wife! All that excessive force against a woman isn't necessary. Plus, that bitch got an ass whooping coming!"

"See, Officer, this is what I was talking about. They are so violent towards me. This is why I fear for my life. Can we please get my kids so I can take them with me to a safe environment?" Carmen had tears streaming down her eyes. This bitch deserved an Oscar for Best Actress in a Hood Movie.

"What the fuck you mean, get your kids? Bitch, them my kids, and you're not taking them anywhere!" I was trying my best to get closer to this bitch but the police was standing in my way.

"Do you have anything showing that they are your children?" the police officer asked.

"No sir, I don't, but this bitch left them on my doorstep over a year ago. Me and my wife have been raising them ever since." In my head, I knew I had fucked up by never signing the birth certificates.

"Sir, I'm sorry we have to remove the children and give them to their legal guardian which is the mother, Carmen Rodriquez."

I looked over at that bitch and she was smirking. She had won and there was nothing I could do at the moment. I felt like a fucking fool.

"Can me and my wife please go in and say goodbye to them?"

"Yeah, I will accompany you."

The officer let Trish out of the handcuffs, we walked into our house, and he followed. Gabriella and Juan were at the kitchen table doing homework. Rosario was fixing dinner.

"Hi Mommy and Daddy. Why are you crying?" Gabriella asked as she wiped tears from our faces.

"Remember when I told you that the woman who tried to take you was your mother but she looked different."

"Yes, Daddy. I remember. She was so mean to us. I don't like her because she hurt Aunt Stacy and Grandma Ammenah." Gabriella started to cry and Trish was holding Juan so tight.

"I'm sorry, but this police officer is here because Carmen is outside and you have to go stay with her but Daddy promises he's coming to get y'all back real soon." I didn't even realize I was crying until I felt the tear fall onto Gabriella's face.

"Do you pinky swear?"

I pinky sweared her and she hugged both me and Trish so tight. Juan was now crying as well.

"Don't cry, Daddy and Mommy. I promise to be a good girl and a good big sister to Juan. I remember what we talked about Daddy. I got this," she said as she went into the closet and grabbed a bag I had put together for them just in case some shit like this happened. It contained clothes, but I hid a cell phone inside in case she needed me. I taught her how to leave the phone on silent and hide it the best way that she could.

"I can't take this!" Trish ran upstairs and slammed the door.

I escorted the kids out and reluctantly handed them over to Carmen. It took everything in me not to pull my heat out and blow her brains out but I had to do this the right way.

"Please, let's work out something out for the sake of them. Can't you see they're hurt behind all of our fighting?"

I didn't care that I was crying like a bitch in front of her. My kids were my life and she was being petty and using them as a pawn in a dangerous ass game.

"Here is the paperwork. We have an appointment at child support court on next Tuesday. Don't be late. The family mediator will be there. Oh yeah, don't bring that bitch with you!"

She placed the kids in the car and they started to drive off. I watched my kids as they beat on the rear window calling for me. All I could do was cry and watch as they disappeared. I turned around and watched as Trish was standing on the balcony connected to our bedroom. I walked into the house and saw Rosario on the couch with Lil Markese. She was crying as well.

"Oh Mr. Markese, I'm so sorry."

"It's okay, Rosario. We're going to get them back. Don't worry about it."

I felt sorry for Rosario because she takes care of the kids day in and day out. She is like family so we all are reeling from this. I hate that I have to call my mother. She is about to spazz the fuck out. I entered our bathroom and Trish had suitcases out packing her clothes.

"Where the fuck are you going?"

"In order for you to be with Gabriella and Juan, I have to be out of the picture. Carmen will never let you breathe peacefully as long as we are together. I'm tired of all this drama. My life has been in shambles since I found out about everything. My shop was the last straw. I have to get away and I need to take my son with me."

"So, all this is about you, Trish? In case you forgot, I have been going through this shit as well. I need you more than anything right now. All I got is you and my son right now. I need you in my corner right now, Ma."

"I'm sorry. I need to get away for a couple of days. I cannot deal with this bullshit right now." She continued to pack as tears fell down her face.

"I hate to admit it but Carmen has us right where she wants us. Right now, I have to play by her rules in order to get my kids back. Don't forget how devious this bitch is. She can put all of us behind bars for the rest of our fucking lives. Obviously, she hasn't said anything about her being buried alive and left for dead. We have to do this shit the right way. I know that you're upset but I need you here with me." I guess she started to think about what I had said because she started to put the clothes back.

"I love you more than you will ever know but I'll be honest with you when I say that I don't think love is enough to keep me here with you. I can't keep putting our son's life in danger because your crazy ass baby momma can't have you. I will walk out that door and leave everything we have if it means that my son would be safe. I need a protector and you're not doing a good job at protecting my heart or my life. I'm going to go spend the night at Aja's house. I'll see you tomorrow afternoon."

Trish walked out the bedroom, grabbed the baby and left. She never gave me a chance to respond. I was speechless and heartbroken. I might have hurt Trish in the past, but I have always been there when she needed me. I feel like everything I have done for her has been in vain. She is being selfish and I don't care what anyone thinks. All the years of hustling and grinding was to make a better life for her and my son. This fucking house didn't just fall from the fucking sky. I put my all into giving her the world and this is the thanks I get?

At this point, I need to be more focused on getting my kids back and the opening of my club. All this bullshit Trish is on is for the birds. Trish has me questioning her loyalty. I need her more than anything and she is basically saying fuck me. For better or for worse my ass. those were the vows we both took. Right now thing have gotten worse and Trish can't handle it.

Chapter 10- Nisa

What's a woman to do when the man she loves, loves another woman? I have tried to deal with it, but I can't. I pray every day that one day I will be enough for Killa. I need to stop praying because God is not listening to my ass. Although Killa called himself coming back to me and trying to make things work that abortion ruined his love for me and I have to deal with it. I wish I could turn back the hands of time. I would have never got that abortion, but it's too late to regret it now. Killa is in a relationship with Remi, the woman from the Ashland Terrace Apartments that he was fucking with. He has moved that bitch in a crib and everything. He comes over to the condo from time to time to drop off money, but that's about it. I never thought that I would be going through this pregnancy alone. Here it is I'm six months pregnant and alone.

I became pregnant the night of the shooting incident. I was so elated when I found out I was pregnant with Killa's baby. It's just crazy that Remi is pregnant as well. He spends way more time with her and that shit hurts like hell. I have come to the conclusion that it's over between us and I have started the healing process. I sit back and think about how I will kill a motherfucker off sight, but I am too weak of a woman to walk away from a marriage that is non-existent.

****

I was trying my best to sleep, but my phone constantly kept ringing. I ignored it as long as I could. I decided to answer it and I was ready to cuss out whoever was calling at four in the damn morning.

"Hello?" I answered sounding pissed.

It was Killa and I was surprised because I haven't heard from him in a month.

"Hey Nisa. Get up and come bail me out of jail. My bond is ten thousand."

"Why are you calling me? Call that bitch Remi. What I look like coming to bond you out and you don't even fuck with me?"

"I don't have time for this shit right now. Are you coming or not, Nisayah?"

"Yeah. I'll be there."

I rolled my ass over and went back to sleep. His ass was going to wait until I got good and goddamn ready to bond him out.

I finally bonded his ass out two days later. I sat outside of my car and watched as he strolled his ass out of the county jail. I rolled my eyes in disgust and watched as he walked towards my car. I thought he would have been mad. Surprisingly, he wasn't.

"Thanks for coming to grab me. I appreciate it." He leaned over and kissed me on the jaw. I wanted to ask what the fuck he got locked up for but decided against it because I didn't even want to care anymore. Even though I really did care.

"How is my son doing?" he asked as he rubbed my belly.

My son immediately started kicking and squirming at the touch of Killa's hand. Most likely because he had never felt it before. Killa has never touched me in the whole six months that I have been pregnant. His touch felt so good. I knew it was only temporary so I knew not to get my hopes up high.

"He's fine. Where do you want to get dropped off?" I asked him first before he got the chance to tell me to drop him off at Remi's house. He had a habit of doing that foul ass shit.

"I'm going to the crib with you."

This nigga was really showing out because I can't remember the last time he stepped a foot inside of our home. Killa was up to something. I just couldn't put my finger on it. I went straight to my room and closed my door. I loved him, but I wasn't about to play this mind game with Killa anymore. He could take his ass to Remi's house. I'm done trying with this marriage. I need to focus on me and my unborn son. If Killa didn't want me anymore then so be it. I refused to play this back and forth game with him.

Chapter 11- Killa

I wonder if I've punished Nisa enough yet. I said to myself.

No matter how hard I try, I just can't get over the fact that this bitch killed my seed. I let go all of my hoes to wife her ass up. I know she's in her feelings about me fucking with Remi, but she shouldn't be because her ass is just somebody I fuck with to pass the time away. I'm through fucking with her though. I went to her crib and walked in on her giving some nigga head. I went ballistic because this bitch is supposed to be pregnant with my seed and disrespecting it like that.

The dude and I exchanged words and that's when I found out that she was really pregnant by him. I lost my cool and smacked fire from her ass. The dude tried to help her so I pistol-whipped him. She immediately called the police. As soon as I drove off in my car, I was pulled over by the police. Now I have a domestic violence and an assault with a deadly weapon case, the last damn thing I need on my rap sheet.

The last couple of months I have been real laid back. It's hard not being in the drug game for me. No matter how much money I have, I want more of that shit. The streets are all a nigga like me knows. I miss the way we had the streets on lock over the years. It pissed me off how we lost it all over one bad decision. I love my team though. I was so engrossed with the street life that I forgot that I owned a couple of residential buildings across the city. I'm checking a bag off of them too. Dealing with my properties on a day-to-day basis has taking up most of my time. I really haven't been dealing with Nisa or the bitch Remi. I have been thinking real hard about my marriage. It's time for me to make this shit right with Nisa. Especially since she is about to give birth to my son. She betrayed me in the worst way by killing my seed, but at the end of the day, she is the only chick that has my heart and my back.

****

"What are you doing?" I asked as I walked into the room and sat down on the bed. I placed her swollen feet on my lap and massaged them.

"Nothing. I'm just trying to figure out why you're here and how long will it be before you leave?" Nisa had her back leaning up against the headboard with a look of sadness in her eyes. At first, her sad ass looks didn't faze me because I hated her ass. Now I'm feeling a little bad about how I've hurt her.

"I'm here because I want to be and I'm here to stay." I placed her toes inside my mouth and sucked on them. She quickly pulled away and sat up straight in the bed.

"There must be trouble in paradise if you're sucking on my toes. You haven't done that in over a year. So, tell me what happened between you and that ratchet ass bitch?"

"That ain't my motherfucking baby, that's what happened!"

"I should have known."

Nisa jumped up and tried to leave out the room. I wasn't about to let her walk out on me while I was trying to make amends. It shouldn't even matter what happened between me and Remi. I'm here with her and that's what's important.

"Look, I'm sorry for my actions. I need you to understand something though. I'm here with you trying to make shit right because I want to. It has nothing to do with Remi. I have my whole new crib and plenty of bitches that would love to be in my presence. I could have called one of the crew to come bail me out. I called you because you're my wife and I need you. You balance me out, Nisa. Let me make this shit right."

I pulled her in close to me and wrapped my arms around her waist. I laid my head on her stomach and she rubbed my head. I felt my son as he kicked me all upside the head. I guess that means he was mad at me too. I raised her shirt up over her head and I stood to my feet. I kissed her soft lips and parted them with my tongue. It had been so long since we made love that I felt like this was our first sexual encounter. We kissed each other passionately and let our hands roam all over each other's body. I took her swollen breasts and began to suck on them. Nisa leaned her head back in pleasure and let light moans escape her mouth. I laid her down on the bed and removed her pants. I kissed her inner thighs and licked my way up to her pussy. I inserted my tongue in and out of her with so much ease. She became dripping wet.

"Oh my God! Killa I missed you so much. Please don't stop. I'm about to cum." As soon as the words left her mouth, I felt her squirting almost as if she was pissing.

"Damn baby, you got that wet-wet!" I stood to my feet and wiped my mouth with the back of my hand.

"I'm sorry it's been a minute for me." Nisa crawled to the edge of the bed as I got undressed. She was tugging at my boxers trying to unleash the beast. I didn't want her to please me though. She deserved to be pleased and pampered.

"Turn around."

I entered her from behind. As soon as I was all the way in, the memories of our sessions flooded my mind. I began to pound inside of her harder and harder. Her pussy felt like Heaven. I got lost in the moment and I was fucking her brains out. I was smacking her on her ass so hard that I was leaving handprints.

"Oh my God, Killa!" Nisa screamed as she gripped the sheets tight and buried her face into the pillow.

"Aargh! Aargh!" I grunted as I came in her. If she weren't already pregnant, she would have definitely been pregnant after this session. Nisa sat up and was holding her stomach.

"What's wrong baby?"

"I think he's just balled up on one side." Nisa was doubled over on the bed holding her stomach. Her ass was scaring me.

"I hope I didn't hurt him. Do you think I was rougher than I should have been?"

"It's okay. Just come here and lay down with me for a minute."

I laid in bed with Nisa and we held each other close. We both drifted off to sleep. Not long after someone banging on the door and leaning on the doorbell woke both of us up. I looked out the window and it was Remi and her sister, Desire. This bitch is only with Remi because I wouldn't let her suck my dick no more. I'm about to catch a murder case because these bitches is about to get murked right on the doorstep. I turned around. Nisa was fully dressed with her Desert Eagle in hand.

"Baby, you're pregnant. Calm down. Let me handle this bitch.

"You better move before I shoot your ass."

Nisa cocked the gun and aimed at me. I had no choice, but to move because she has wanted to put a hole in my ass since I laid hands on her for killing my seed. Nisa ran down the stairs two at a time. I watched as she swung the door open and pointed her gun at them.

"If you two bitches don't get the fuck away from my crib, I will blow you bitches brains out."

"Tell Killa to bring his bitch ass out. If he thinks he's not going to take care of this baby, he got me fucked all up."

"Your ugly ass already fucked up. Killa, you need to handle this shit. Let her know what's really good."

"Remi gon' head on with that bullshit. It's a wrap. I caught your ass in a lie and I'm not fucking with you anymore."

I slammed the door in her face and then I heard glass breaking. This bitch had busted Nisa's windshield in her car. Nisa ran out the door and pounced on Remi's ass. The shit happened so fast that I didn't have time to grab Nisa before she hit Remi's ass. They started to fight and I managed to pull them apart, but not before Remi was able to kick Nisa in the stomach. She went down like a ton of bricks and that's when I saw the fluid mixed with blood running down her legs.

"Bitch, you might as well leave town," I said through gritted teeth. She ran and jumped in her car and sped off so fast.

"Call the ambulance! I feel like he's trying to come out. I feel the urge to push!"

"We don't have time for that. I'll have to take you myself."

I ran to garage and pulled my Escalade Truck around. I lifted her into the passenger seat. I drove like a bat out of hell. I knew this shit was going to turn out bad.

"I'm so sorry Nisa. Baby, please forgive me."

"It's okay. Just get me to the hospital. I feel like I'm about to pass out. This shit hurts like hell."

We hadn't even made it all the way inside the hospital. Nisa gave birth to my son in the emergency entrance. He was so tiny that he could fit in the palm of your hand. He wasn't breathing at all. We weren't able to kiss or hold him before they rushed him to the Neonatal Intensive Care Unit. We were both sad as fuck. I cried so fucking hard seeing my little nigga like that.

The doctor's told us to prepare ourselves just in case he didn't make it. What type of shit is that to tell parents who just gave birth? I was sick and murder was on my mind. That bitch was dying pregnant and all. I was glad when I walked out to the waiting area. The whole crew was there as always. No matter what happens, we have each other's back in times such as this. I needed them now more than ever. I was already pissed the fuck off at Remi. I went from pissed to livid in a matter of seconds as I watched Carmen come through the emergency room doors.

Chapter 12- Carmen

Ever since I took the kids from Markese and Trish, Juan had been running a high fever. I went and brought over the counter drugs, but nothing worked for him. His fever had gotten up to one hundred and three degrees. I knew I had to take him into the emergency room. I wanted to call Markese. I didn't have time for him to curse me out and tell me how bad of a mother I was. I was actually bonding with the kids. At first, they were scared of me, but I got them to become more relaxed around me. This time with them has made me regret everything I have put them through.

Once we arrived to the emergency room, I walked up to the receptionist and gave Juan's information. I filled out some paperwork and had a seat in the waiting area. It was only then I realized Markese and the crew was sitting on the other side. I tried to get up and walk away, but the blow I felt to the back of my head let me know I hadn't walked away fast enough.

"Really bitch? I have been waiting to see you. Did you think you could get away with shooting me and my fucking mother?"

Stacy was raining blows on me. One after another. I didn't even get a chance to swing back. The next thing I knew, I was on the ground being stomped and beaten. I knew that it was Aja, Niyah, and Trish who had joined in on the beating. All I could do was ball up and cover my face. These hoes were actually stomping me with heels on.

"Okay! Okay! That's enough," Markese said as he pulled Trish off of me. The hospital security was also grabbing the other girls.

"Let me the fuck go! This is the second time you have pulled me off this bitch when I was whooping her ass. You know this bitch burned down my shop! This bitch has destroyed our lives and you're still protecting her!"

I had finally got up from the floor and I was bleeding from my lip and my nose.

"I don't care about you beating her ass. Don't ya'll see Gabriella and Juan sitting right here. There's a place and time for everything." Markese sat down on the bench and hugged the kids.

"Why is it that every time ya'll come to this hospital, it's drama. If you all cannot control yourselves I will have you permanently banned," the security guard spoke. He directed his words to the crew.

"I want to off this bitch so bad right now!" Rahmeek said through gritted teeth.

He started kicking the garbage cans over and throwing chairs around the waiting room. He was escorted out by the security guards. I watched as Killa, Hassan, and Boogie gave me death stares. I hate Markese, but if he wouldn't have come to my rescue, I would be dead right now.

"I'm officially done with your shit, Markese! As for you, bitch this is far from over. We're boxing every time we see each other. Please keep on your Nikes."

Trish walked away and the rest of the crew exited as well. In the end, it was just Markese and our kids in the waiting area.

"What's wrong with him?"

"I don't know. He has had a fever for a couple of days. I have tried everything and nothing has worked. That's why I brought him in."

"You should have called and said something."

"For what? So that you could tell me how bad of a mother I was? Or so you and your people could kill me?"

Markese was quiet because he knew I was telling the truth. After a while, they called Juan's name. We both went back and sat while he was seen by the doctor. Juan had a severe ear infection. The doctor sent him home with pain meds and antibiotics. I allowed Markese to say goodbye to the kids and we went our separate ways. I observed how much he loved our kids.

Once we made it back to the house, I noticed how sad they had become since leaving the hospital. I came to the conclusion that it was best that they be with their father. The last thing I wanted was for them to be unhappy with me. All this shit I have been doing has really fucked up my life. I'm officially done with trying to ruin Markese's life. As a matter fact, I think I just need to leave Chicago and start over fresh in another state. In order for me to move on with my life, I have to let go of all things that hurt me in the past.

Chapter 13 -Markese

Since Carmen took the kids, I have been depressed. Seeing them today made me feel better. I was glad she didn't clown after the girls whooped her ass. I actually let them get that ass good before I stopped the fight. I noticed Gabriella and Juan getting upset so I stepped in. The whole crew was upset behind my actions. Once I made it back to the crib, I called a quick meeting with everyone. Killa needed to get back to the hospital to be with his son and Nisa. I sat at the head of the table as usual. I reminisced as I watched everyone come in and take their usual seats. It was then I realized how much I missed the crew. I observed Trish throwing daggers at me. At this point, I really didn't give a fuck. Her walking out on me when Carmen came and got the kids has me feeling like she isn't worthy of being my wife.. I needed her support and she just bailed. That shit really hurt me.

"I know everyone is upset and on edge at the fact that Carmen was right there and we couldn't get at her. I only stopped the fight because the kids were present."

"Could have fooled the shit out of me." Trish was really trying to piss me off. I ignored her and continued to talk.

"As you all know Carmen has the kids in her custody. There is nothing that I can do about it. She is their legal guardian. She has me by the balls and I have to play by her rules if I ever want my kids back. "

"That's the fucking problem, Markese. we have been playing by her rules for the longest. I'm tired of this shit and I don't know how much more I can take. That bitch burned down my shop and you're not doing shit about it."

"I told you that I would build you another shop. I need you to be patient. My kids come first at this point." I wasn't trying to be selfish to her feelings. If it was Lil Markese, I would choose him first as well.

"Those kids are the reason why our relationship is the way it is."

I wanted to smack the shit out of her right in front of everyone in the room. I held my composure, but I was at her ass once the meeting was over.

"I need everyone to follow my lead. I got this shit in the bag."

"Don't worry, Kese. We all can agree that we want you to get the kids back. You need to hit us up though if shit gets funky. Hassan and I will finish getting everything ready for the grand opening," Rahmeek said and everyone else agreed in unison, minus Trish. She got up and walked out of the conference room slamming the door behind her. I got up to follow her but Aja grabbed me before I made it to the door.

"She's just upset right now, Kese. Don't be mad at her." Aja said as I got ready to go behind her.

"Mind your own business, Aja!"

I snatched away from her and went to find Trish. The last thing I wanted was to hear some shit from Aja. I need to make it a priority to holler at her about her recent behavior. I didn't raise a hoe and her fucking Marlo in her brother- in law's house was some straight up hoe shit. I looked around the house and found her in the kitchen sitting at the table drinking a glass of wine. I walked over to her and knocked the glass from her hand.

"What the fuck is wrong with you, Trish?"

"Nigga, you don't give a fuck about me or our son with your selfish ass. All you're worried about is Gabriella and Juan. I love them, but I have to admit that had they not been born I would be happy." Trish was slurring, but a drunk person speaks a sober mind.

In my heart, I didn't want to believe that she hated my kids. My anger got the best of me and I yanked her ass up and slammed her into the wall. I put my forearm in her throat to keep her from moving

"Bitch, are you saying you hate my kids?"

"No. I love them and you know that. I love you, but my life has been hell since all this bullshit you created. I'm tired of fighting for this shit."

"It's funny how I'm the selfish one, but you're showing your selfishness right now. I fucked up, Trish. Those are my children and nothing will ever change that. What's fucking me up is that you wait until I need you the most to show how disloyal you are. I have busted my ass giving you the world and this is the thanks I get. I never thought you would become an ungrateful bitch. If you tired of fighting so am I. I'm done with your ass. Get the fuck out, but you leave my son here!"

"I'm not going anywhere. This is my house as well as it is yours. If you want me out, I suggest you take me the court. I guess it's safe to say we're done. I'll move into the guest bedroom. Do you because I'm definitely about to do me."

It took everything in me not to beat her ass. I was going to give her exactly what she wanted though. When I got through doing me, she would regret she ever told me to do the shit.

****

It had been a week since Trish and I decided to officially end our relationship. We both came to an agreement that we didn't want a divorce. Separation was the best thing for us now. I moved out and let her have the house. I bought it for her anyway. I had purchased a condo on the Gold Coast in downtown Chicago. I couldn't believe she just gave up on us like that. No matter what foul shit I have done to her, she has always had my heart and my soul.

The last thing I ever wanted was to lose the love of my life. Trish would usually cry when we had a fallen out like this. That's how I know it's really over. She didn't shed a tear once. Her facial expression was serious as hell. I'm just respecting her wishes and moving on. I hate that my baby boy is in the middle. As a man, I have to get better at being a father. My kids are always in the middle of my fuck-ups.

Carmen had been calling me for the last couple of days. I ignored her because I didn't want any contact with her until our meeting. It was postponed due to our judge being out sick. Finally, the time had come for us to meet up with the family liaison. At the last minute, I received a text from her saying to meet her at our old house. That bitch had been living there the whole time. I pulled into the driveway and Carmen was standing on the porch.. Her usually feisty and unstable demeanor was gone. I walked on the porch and she handed me some papers.

"What's this?"

"It's custody of the kids. I gave up my parental rights to them. They deserve to be with you." Tears were streaming down her face. That shit surprised me because I haven't seen her cry since the day I walked out on her ass.

"What are you up to, Carmen? Since when do you cry or be nice to me for that matter?"

"Too much time has passed for Gabriella and Juan to ever look at me like a mother again. Regardless of me hating Trish, they love her. She has been more of a mother to them than I ever could be. If I could go back, I would have just accepted the fact that you no longer wanted me. My father would be alive and I would still have my kids."

I stood there speechless because I never felt an ounce of guilt for leaving her. I can admit that I treated her better than a sideline, but I had also used her to stay close with her pops. She was beneficial to my rise to the top. She had nothing but love for me and I fumbled her heart by making her think she was more to me than she really was.

"I know it's too late, Carmen, however, I'm sorry for hurting you."

"It's cool it doesn't hurt as much now as it used to. I fell in love with someone else's man. I thought that if I did everything you asked me to, you would leave Trish for me eventually. Things didn't work out in my favor. All the hatred I have for you has cost me my entire family. Please take care of them for me. When they're older, tell them how good I was before I abandoned them and caused all the chaos. For the record, I never stopped loving you, Markese. I just couldn't let you live happy with her. As far as Rahmeek goes, he was just a pawn in my evil twisted game. I'm sorry for everything."

Carmen walked into the house, grabbed the kids, and walked them out on the porch to me. She bent down on her knees to kiss them both and hug them tight.

"I love you both with all my heart. I'm sorry for everything. No matter what I've done, Please understand I did it for the love of you."

I was speechless at the sight before me. The old Carmen was standing in front of me despite the change in appearance. She walked in the house and closed the door. I grabbed my kids and got the fuck out of dodge. I took them to my apartment. They begged to go see Trish and their little brother. I really wanted to take them, but the words Trish spoke about them made me not want them around her ass at all.

Chapter 14-Trish

Never in a million years did I think that Markese and I would be separated from one another. I would be lying if I said I didn't love or miss him because I do. I just couldn't continue dealing with the drama that Carmen was causing in our lives. That bipolar ass bitch burned down my shop. I know she did. My shop was everything to me. I put my all into building my brand, only for that bitch to come along and take it all away with the flick of a match. I blame Markese for all of this shit. I'm sick and tired of always putting my feelings on the backburner. I have followed his lead and held our family together for the longest, despite his indiscretions. I love Gabriella and Juan those are my children. I regret making the statement about them. However, I'm just tired of Markese and all of the extra baggage that comes along with him. I've been a little depressed lately behind our breakup. He is all I have known since I was fourteen years old. How does a woman get over a breakup such as this?

Lately, I have been texting and talking on the phone with the guy I met at Lalo's. Yasir is really cool and funny. He keeps asking to take me out, but I'm not ready for that just yet. I'm not ready to be dealing with another man this fast. I was honest about my feelings and I glad he respected that.

I had been dreading attending the opening of Markese's new club, but I really wanted to support Rahmeek and Hassan. It would also give me a chance to kick it with my girls. We haven't been in touch lately and I wanted to keep it that way. The grand opening of the club was tonight and I was running late as hell. I was dressed in an all white Gucci dress with a pair of Red Bottoms. I was trying something new with my hair. I was rocking a twenty-inch fire red sew-in with a Chinese bang. I flat ironed it and it was pretty as hell. I couldn't wait to make an entrance and shut some shit down.

The line to get inside the club was wrapped around the corner. There was a red carpet and photographers taking pictures as guests entered the club. As I walked down the red carpet, I spotted the girls taking their picture. I rushed towards the front so that I could get in the picture.

"Look at you, bitch. You're rocking that red hair!" Aja said as she ran her hands threw it.

"Yeah, that shit's hot," Niyah added as we gathered together and took the picture.

We entered the club and the shit was off the chain. Markese and the guys had really outdone themselves. The first level was a bar and grill where you could sit down and eat. As we went up to the second level, I was in awe of all the strippers. The entire floor gave off the effect of shining diamonds. These women were beautiful. They were dancing inside cages, working the poles, and the niggas was making it rain on all of the women.

"I need to step my game up if my husband is going to be around all this pussy," Niyah said.

"Girl, you don't have to worry about Hassan. On the other hand, I should be the one stepping my game up. We all know my husband has the worst track record," Aja said as she applied lip-gloss to her lips.

"Let's go up to VIP so we can get our drink on," Stacy said as she walked ahead of us.

We followed her to the VIP section. As we all walked in, the guys were drinking and toasting. I was surprised and kind of glad Markese hadn't arrived yet. I sat down and ordered a Patron margarita. I watched the strippers in amazement as they swung from the ceiling in swings. The shit was off the chain. I was really trying not to pay attention to Niyah, Aja, and Stacy because they were all booed up with their husbands. Of course, Nisa and Killa weren't in attendance due to the birth of the baby. He's doing a little better, but not as well as the doctors want him to be.

About twenty minutes later, Markese walked into the VIP with the biggest smile ever and a date on his arm. My heart dropped in my shoes. I couldn't believe he actually brought a date to the grand opening. He knew I would be here. I had to put my game face on and not show my hurt or my anger. The crew was looking all bewildered and crazy at him and me.

"This is nice ass turn out ya'll," he said as he popped a bottle of Ace of Spades and poured his date a glass.

"Aren't you going to introduce us to your friend?" Aja asked with a slight attitude.

"I'm sorry lil sis. This is my girl, Nadia."

Every one spoke and she spoke back to them. She was real pretty. She looked like she was mixed with Mexican or something. She and Markese had the nerve to be dressed in all white. I was hating him and this bitch even more. I hated to admit it, but they looked so good together.

"I'm sorry. I didn't get your name."

This bitch had her hand out to shake mine. I looked at her ass like she had two fucking heads.

"I'm Trish, Markese's wife."

I shook her hand and sipped my drink. The look on her face was priceless. She looked over at him with a disappointed look on her face. The crew sat around speechless as hell.

"We're separated, right?" Markese asked me as he drank straight from the bottle.

"You damn right motherfucker!"

I threw my drink in his face and rushed out of the VIP section. He tried to get up and come after me, but I was too fast for his ass. I wanted to cry so bad. I know that I am the one who wanted to end things. I didn't anticipate he would move on so fucking fast. I walked into the bathroom and looked in the mirror. Seeing him with another woman crushed me. I felt my phone vibrating. When I retrieved it from my purse, it was a text from Yasir.

What are you doing? I was at a party, but I'm getting ready to leave.
Let me come scoop you. I need to see your beautiful face.
Okay. I'll be outside the entrance of Gentlemen's Paradise.
I'll be there in five minutes.

Despite being scared shitless about kicking it with him, I agreed to go. Markese had moved on. There was no reason why I should sit around and cry about our relationship any longer. I exited the bathroom, went to the bar, and ordered me another Patron margarita. I was already tipsy from the first one so I knew this second would have me real nice. About five minutes later, Yasir texted that he was outside. I exited the club and he was sitting outside in a cocaine white Aston Martin. This nigga had to be caked the fuck up. He got out and opened the car door for me.

"Hey beautiful. You're rocking the shit out of that dress, Ma."

"Thank you. You're not looking too bad yourself."

Yasir was dressed in an all white linen suit with a pair of white Air Force Ones. His hair was pulled back into a ponytail. His hair was draping down his back. This nigga was fine as hell. As Yasir walked back around to the driver's side of the car, I looked at the club entrance and Markese was standing in the doorway. He was watching me like a hawk. He had murder in his eyes and I didn't give a fuck. Ain't no fun when the rabbit got the gun. I laughed at his ass as we drove away.

My phone instantly started ringing and texting. I knew it was
Markese. I reached inside my purse and shut the power button off. He was
not about to ruin my first night with Yasir. He was with that bitch anyway.
I was unsure of where Yasir was taking me. I didn't want to seem like I
was worried although I was. I guess he sensed my uneasiness. He reached
over and placed his hand on my leg. His hand felt so good and soft. My
panties were getting wet instantaneously. The mixture of liquor and
looking at his fine ass had a bitch horny as fuck. Not to mention it's been a
minute since I had some dick.

"What's on your mind, Ma? Talk to me."

"I'm good. I just have some things going on with my husband.
nothing major."

"That was him giving me the death stare back there?"

I had no idea he had even peeped Markese in the doorway. "Yeah,
that was him. I'm sorry about that. He's just mad because I was with you. I
really don't know why because he came with some chick named Nadia."
There was awkward silence for a minute before he spoke up.

"Don't worry about that shit. Tonight, it's all about you. If it's okay, I
would like to take you to my condo and cater to you."

He rubbed his fingers threw my hair and it felt so good. I was about to
let go of all my inhibitions. We were both free agents so there was no need
for me to continue holding back from him.

"I'm cool with that." He grabbed my hand and our fingers
intertwined. He brought my hand up to his lips and placed a kiss on it with
his soft, pink, and juicy lips. I had to cross my legs. I just knew juices
would be running down my legs at any minute. After driving for about
another ten minutes we ended up in front of a beautiful gated community
filled with luxurious condos. We pulled into the garage and went into the

house. it was nice and simple. It looked barely lived in. It was then I remembered he had told me lived here and in Miami.

"Make yourself at home. I'm going to make you some bathwater." I sat down on the couch and removed my shoes. I pulled out my phone and powered it on. All the text messages Markese had sent started to come through. I opened it and read the last incoming message.

So that's why your ass wanted to end shit. You have been fucking with dude all along. I should have known with your sneaky pussy ass. You better stay the fuck away from me. Real Talk. If you know like I know you better not have that bitch ass nigga around my son. On everything I love if I find out he been near my house or my son Imma put a bullet in both of ya'll motherfucking heads. Disloyal ass bitch.

I wished that I had never opened up the damn text. Tears were falling down my face and falling onto the screen.

"Your water is ready."

I got up and made sure to wipe my face so that he wouldn't see the tears falling. For the rest of the night, Yasir catered to me. He bathed me, rubbed lotion all over my body, and gave me the best massage ever. His hands felt good all over my body. I fell asleep in his bed. The next morning when I woke up, he wasn't next to me. I got up and went downstairs and he was cooking breakfast.

"Good morning, sleepy head." He grabbed a plate and started placing eggs, grits, sausages, and toast on it.

"Thank you so much, Yasir. I'm so sorry I fell asleep on you."

"It's cool, Ma. I kind of liked hearing you snore." We both laughed and we sat down and ate breakfast.

"It's getting late. I need to get my son from his grandparents' house."

"I know we just met, but I would really love to take you to Miami for the weekend. You can bring the baby if you would like."

"I don't know about that, Yasir. I'll let you know before the day is out."

Yasir dropped me back off to my car that I left at the club overnight. I stopped by my house and changed my clothes before I picked up my baby. It was twelve in the afternoon. I felt bad for leaving the baby on Momma Gail and Mike like that. I was supposed to pick him up at nine this morning. I pulled up to their house and noticed Markese's car parked outside. I had to mentally prepare myself for the shit he was about to pull. Before I could even get out the car to knock on the door, he came out of the door and charged towards me. He grabbed my arm and dragged me towards the door like I was child who had did something wrong.

"You like that nigga that much that you forgot to pick our son up on time?"

"I didn't forget about him, Markese. I overslept."

"That nigga must have had his dick up in you and down your throat all night. Ol' hoe ass."

"I don't have time for this shit. You were the same one that was with a bitch last night. So don't come at me talking crazy about who I fuck and suck on. We're separated, remember. Now let me get my baby so that we can bounce.

"Fuck all that shit you talking about. Don't get your ass whooped talking out the side of your neck." Markese mushed me in the head so hard that it hit the corner of the doorway causing blood to seep out instantly. "Oh shit, Trish. I'm sorry. I didn't mean to do that."

"Get your fucking hands off of me!" I walked inside and grabbed my baby quick as hell.

"Mommy! Mommy! We missed you."

Gabriella and Juan were hugging me so tight. I cried because I truly missed them. Markese never even told me he had them.

"You have blood on your head, Mommy," Juan said as he hugged me around the waist.

Markese came from the back holding a towel and he handed it to me. Momma Gail and Mike came into the house and noticed the blood.

"Mommy's bleeding, Grandma."

Gail came over towards me and examined my head. "How did this happen?"

He looked at Markese and me as she asked the question.

"Daddy was mad at her, but he didn't mean it." Gabriella said as she wrapped her arms around his waist.

"I'm so tired of all this drama with this family I don't know what to do. Mike, take Trish to the hospital. I'll deal with our son."

I was so embarrassed and ashamed. As soon as I got my head looked at, I was getting my baby and hopping on that plane to Miami with Yasir. I needed to get far away from Markese.

Chapter 15- Momma Gail

I love my kids more than life itself. I thank God everyday for bringing us back together. Since I've been clean, our family bond has strengthened. These last two years have been full of drama. I truly don't know how much more I can take. I sit in the background and mind my business because my kids are grown. I just want to be supportive and help raise my grandchildren. I'm glad that I have Mike. He keeps me grounded and sane. Since his retirement, he has been trying to get me to move to Virginia. I kept telling him I wasn't ready because I couldn't leave the kids. I have been rethinking that decision though. My blood pressure is through the roof dealing with Markese and Aja's never ending relationship bullshit. Coming inside the house and seeing Trish bleeding pissed me off. I already knew that Markese had put his hands on her before, but in my house and in front of these damn kids was where I drew the line. Markese was sitting on the couch holding Lil Markese as he slept.

"Why would you put your hands on her like that?"

"Ma I'm sorry. It truly was an accident."

"Accident, my ass! Please miss me with the bullshit! What the hell is going on with ya'll now?"

"We both agreed that we would separate. I wasn't really feeling it, but she said that she was tired of all the bullshit with Carmen. I was mad, but I had to respect her wishes. So, last night at the club opening I brought a date with me just to fuck with her. The broad ain't shit to me. Trish got mad and threw a drink in my face. I went to look for her and found her outside getting in the car with some nigga."

"Let me guess. Seeing her with another man pissed you off, huh?"

"Yeah. All I could think of was him touching my wife. She belongs to me and no other nigga."

I couldn't do shit but laugh at this fool I gave birth to. The look on his face let me know that he was dead ass serious.

"Damn Ma. It's like that? How you going be laughing when we having a serious conversation?"

I immediately stopped laughing and put my serious face on. I had to spit knowledge to my son. He had life fucked all the way up if he thought it was okay to think he could do the bullshit he had done to Trish and get away with it.

"I love you Markese, but if she was with another man, you brought it on yourself. That girl was with you when I was strung out on that shit. I remember her and her momma taking care of you and Aja. She loved you when you didn't have shit. She loves your kids despite the fact that you cheated on her and had them. They are a constant reminder of your lies and deceit. Let's not forget their psychotic ass mother who has terrorized this family. I'm sorry, but that shit is your fault. Not to mention you had the nerve to have a DNA test done on that baby knowing he was yours. Trish loves her shop. It being burned down like that took a lot out of her. She came over here crying about you not being supportive enough when she needs you. That's why she is out with another man. You're not giving her what she needs to be happy." He just sat there looking stupid as hell. Markese knew I was telling the truth.

"So what do you suggest I do to get my wife back?"

"I suggest you start treating your wife like a Queen and not like some bitch on the street that you're just fucking. Get your shit together before it's too late. Take your kids home. I need some alone time with your Daddy, If you get my drift."

We both laughed and I kissed him on the forehead and left him sitting there. Next on my agenda is hot pussy ass Aja around here fucking and kissing her ex. That shit makes no sense at all to me. She knows better than to get mixed up with Marlo's psycho ass.

Chapter 16-Aja

The grand opening of the club was epic. I am so proud of my husband and my brother. Speaking of my brother, this nigga has officially lost his mind bringing some random bitch around us. I'm not sure what's going on with Trish and my brother but the shit has got to stop. I have been calling Trish all night without an answer. I called Markese and he was at Gail's house. I wasn't really feeling her and her attitude with me lately. I already know it's about the Marlo situation. That was a one-time thing. That shit will never happen again. I have moved back in the house with Rahmeek. Things are going good. However, Marlo is constantly calling and texting me. I had to put his ass on the block list. I just pray that Marlo gets the picture and leave me alone. His stupid ass gon' get us both killed.

I walked inside my mother's living room and observed Markese on the couch with all his kids. He looked pitiful as hell. Served his ass right for flaunting that bitch in Trish face.

"Hey big bro."

"What's up lil sis?"

"Shit. I'm worried about you and Trish. What's going on with ya'll?"

Markese rubbed his hand over his goatee and laid his head back on the couch. "She's fucking with another nigga. I saw her get in his car last night. She stayed out all night with that nigga. We're not even living in the same house anymore. It's like she hates me. That's some shit I can't deal with."

I was speechless because this is the first I heard of them not being together. Markese looked like shit. I really felt sorry for him. I sat beside him on the couch and rested my head on his shoulder. Despite being older and married, I'm still a baby around my big brother. I could be mad at him one minute and all under him the next.

"Everything will be okay. You know how Trish gets when she is mad at you. I'll talk with her."

"Thanks, lil sis."

He kissed me on the forehead and that's when my Momma walked in the living room with her hands on her hips. *Here we go with this shit.* I thought to myself

"I'm going to cut straight to the chase. Did you have sex with that fool Marlo in Niyah's house?"

"Yeah Momma. It won't happen again."

I put my head down in shame because Markese had a disappointed look on his face. "I'm sorry Markese. I was just upset about everything going on with Rahmeek. If it's any consolation, Hassan told Rahmeek. We have talked about it and it's over. We're good, Ma. So please stop worrying about me."

"Baby girl, you don't get it. I'm worried about Marlo. We all know how crazy that nigga was about you. He would shoot a nigga if they looked at you wrong. He's fucking with Rahmeek now. Marlo ain't ready for the noise my son-in-law will bring his ass. So, if he knows like I know he better breathe easy and stay away from you. Or should I be saying that you need to stay your hot pussy ass away from him?" Markese nodded and agreed with my mother. I laughed at both them.

"Momma I always knew you were Team Rah."

"You damn right. He might fuck up from time to time. However, he's a provider and loves his family. That's my son-in-law no matter what."

As soon as I got ready to respond, Trish and Mike walked through the door. I wanted to say something, but the look in her eyes said now was not the time. Trish walked in and snatched the baby from Markese and walked right out of the door. She slammed the door so hard she knocked a couple of pictures off of the wall.

"Damn! You done fucked up now, son," Mike said as he and my mother walked to the back of the house. I thought that Markese would go behind her but he didn't. He just sat there looking like a fool.

"Are you going to just sit here and let her go?"

"Yep. I hurt Trish and she ain't feeling me right now. I'm going to give her the space she wants. Let me get my kids to the crib."

Markese got up and left. Over the years, they have fallen out plenty of times but nothing like this. I truly believe it may be over. I hope and pray that it isn't over between them. I would feel like a little girl whose parents are getting a divorce. They have both practically raised me. I need to talk with Trish. Hopefully, I can get through to her before this shit gets more out of hand than it already is. I made it to Trish's house about an hour later. I was getting ready to park when I saw a fine ass Mexican man carrying my fucking nephew. He placed him in the back of the car in his car seat and he got into the driver's seat. A couple of minutes later, Trish emerged from the house carrying some bags. I hopped out the car and walked towards her.

"What the fuck is going on, Trish? Who is that nigga holding my nephew?"

"Look Aja, not right now. I need to get away lil sis. I promise I'll be back on Monday. We can talk about everything then, okay?"

She hugged me and got inside the car. I was flabbergasted as I stood there watching her drive away. I'm just glad Markese didn't see that nigga holding his son. It definitely would have been some bloodshed. I turned around to get in my car and that's when I saw Marlo leaning against his Benz. *I know this nigga is not stalking me,* I said to myself. I walked towards my car and tried to get in, but he blocked me. I tried pushing him out of the way.

"Move Marlo. I need to get home and get my son!"

"You think you can just fuck my brains out and leave me hanging." He caressed the side of my face and I moved my face away.

"I told you that shit was a mistake. I'm back with my husband. Please, Marlo, stop calling me and following me before shit gets real for you. Rahmeek don't play this shit that you're pulling."

"You, out of everybody, know I'm not scared of your bitch ass husband. He bleeds just like I do. At the end of the day, I was your first. I'll be your last and everything after that. Get with the fucking program, Aja."

He kissed me on the lips and walked away from me. I was so damn happy he drove away. On the ride home, I contemplated telling Rahmeek about our encounter. I was scared because lately his temper has been through the roof. He has been overwhelmed with the club. The last thing I need to do was add to his stress. He would be pissed if he found out from someone else and not me. We have been doing good since we decided to make this shit work. Marlo's psycho ass ain't worth me fucking up with my husband. It would be in my best interest to tell him. I don't need him laying hands on my ass. I'm still feeling the after effects of him slapping my ass the last time.

The smell of greens and smoked turkey tails could be smelled as soon as I pulled into the driveway of our house. I entered the kitchen and immediately went towards the stove. Rahmeek was cooking dressing, baked macaroni, candy yams, greens, and roast. It had been a minute since he got down in the kitchen. I was glad he cooked because my stomach was in my back. I searched the house and found Rahmeek and this bitch

Karima sitting in my living room on my damn couch. I looked at them like they both had lost their minds.

"They released your ass, huh?" I asked with a smirk on my face.

"Yes. I'm so glad. I just stopped by to tell you and Rahmeek how much I appreciate ya'll taking care of her while I was away. From the bottom of my heart I really appreciate you."

"It's all good. We love Lil Momma."

"Well let me get her home. I have to be in before ten at night. We will stick to the same schedule. I'll make sure to have her back to you guys on the weekend."

"It's cool, Karima. You can have her this weekend so that you all can get reacquainted."

Karima and Brooklyn walked out of the door and I could tell Rahmeek was missing his little girl already. He stood in the doorway and watched as she drove away. I hugged him around the waist and kissed his neck. We closed the door and headed back inside.

"So, what's up with the feast in the kitchen?"

"Nothing major. I just wanted to cook dinner for my family for a change. Now go set the table and wake up Lil Rah from his nap. He thinks he can sleep all day and be up all night cockblocking his pops. I need to make love to you tonight," Rahmeek spoke to me as he went inside the kitchen and turned off the pots.

"How come you can't make love to me right now?" I walked towards him and dropped down to my knees. I unbuckled his belt and unleashed the beast. I placed it in my hot and wet mouth. I methodically sucked and slurped on it hungrily.

Rahmeek grabbed the back of my head and guided my head up and down on his dick. As soon as he came in my mouth, I heard Lil at the top of the stairs calling out for us. "

"I told you he's a cockblocker."

We both laughed as he fixed his pants and went to get Lil Rah. Once I set the table and we sat down to eat. I knew now was the best time to tell Rah about Marlo.

"I need to tell you something, but I don't want you to get upset and go ballistic." I couldn't even look at him in his face because I was scared like I had done something wrong. I just kept staring down at my plate of food. Rahmeek was staring me down like a hawk.

"I don't have time for all this stalling Aja. We're back on the right track. Now what the fuck do you have to tell me?"

"Lately, Marlo has been calling and texting my phone. I never answered his calls or responded to his texts. I ended up putting him on the block list. Today, he followed me to my mother's house. I told him what happened between us was a mistake. I told him that we were back together. He basically started talking about how he's not scared of you and I belonged to him."

Rahmeek got up from his chair and flipped the whole table over. I jumped up and grabbed Lil Rah because started to cry.

"Calm down, Rahmeek!"

"What the fuck you mean, calm down? That nigga talking all reckless and shit. I'm about to fuck dude up."

He walked out the door without even looking back. I knew I shouldn't have said shit. I will be blamed for whatever happens between him and Marlo. I wanted to go after him, but I knew that was a bad idea. I cleaned up all of the food he knocked on the floor and went to bed. I really wish I never told him. I can only imagine what he has done to Marlo.

Chapter 17- Rahmeek

The fact that this bitch made ass nigga think it's okay to disrespect me has me livid. I did beyond the fucking speed limit headed towards Hassan and Niyah's crib. I pulled in their driveway at the same time that Marlo's bitch ass did. I went inside my glove compartment and grabbed my Desert Eagle. I exited the car and walked towards his ass full speed. That nigga never seen me coming when he exited his vehicle. I didn't come over here to do no talking. I cocked backed my hammer and let loose. I hit his ass in both legs. He yelled out in pain as I stood over his ass in the driveway.

"Bitch ass nigga, I don't know if you need Hooked on Phonics or what. Stay away from my fucking wife. That shit between ya'll is over. I just gave your bitch ass was a warning. I'm aiming for your dome Next time. I spared your ass out of love for Niyah, but keep testing me and that shit will go out of the window." I kicked his bitch ass in the face and left his ass leaking in the driveway.

****

It was about eight in the morning the next day when I heard Niyah banging on our front door. Aja jumped up and went to open the door. I was right behind her I knew Niyah was pissed off at me.

"Why are you banging on the door like that this early in the morning? Is everything okay, bestie?

"Get that fake ass shit out of my face, Aja! You know damn well everything is not okay. Your husband came to my house yesterday and shot my brother in both of his legs."

Aja turned around and looked at me with a shocked look on her face. I really don't know why she was shocked. She already knows I'm about that gunplay. I just sat down on the couch and waited for Niyah to finish her rant.

"Actually, I didn't know shit. So, I'm going to need you to stop disrespecting me in my fucking house. I understand your upset about Marlo, but that nigga was stalking me so I told my husband."

"Bitch please! What the fuck did you think would happen, Aja? You fucked my brother the first night he came home from jail. You know damn well how Marlo is about you. I'm sorry but I have no sympathy for your sneaky pussy ass. I'm not saying that Marlo was right for following or constantly calling you after you asked him not to. However, you are not innocent in all of this."

"Bitch, I never said I was innocent. As a matter of fact, I'm not about to go back and forth with you about this, Niyah. You're my friend and the last thing I want is for us to beef.

"I'm not sure I want to be friends with your selfish ass anymore. You think the world revolves around Aja. You never think about the consequences behind your actions. Let me enlighten you on some shit. Just like you love Markese, I love Marlo. Don't get it twisted, I will go hard for my blood right or wrong. If it means losing you as a friend and Hassan as a husband, then so be it. As for you, Rahmeek, I'm not fucking with you at all period. Stay away from me and my kids. I mean that shit. You disrespected me and put my kids in danger yesterday. This is the last straw for me. You two belong together with ya'll dysfunctional asses."

"There is no need for you to disrespect Aja. I'm the one you're mad at. Get all that shit off of your chest your feeling. I really don't give a fuck. I'm going to tell you like I told your bitch ass brother, next time I'm aiming for his dome!"

"Your ass is not the only one who knows how to use a gun. That shit goes both ways. I'm done with ya'll," Niyah said as she walked back to her car.

Aja was standing there crying. I felt sorry for her because she and Niyah are thick ass thieves. At the same damn time, this shit was bound to happen. My only concern now is my relationship with Hassan. He loves Niyah just like I love Aja, but before we had wives, all we had was each other. Shit, only time will tell.

Chapter 18- Hassan

All this bullshit that was going on had me pissed the fuck off. I knew the moment, Niyah's brother walked into my house he was going to be a problem. Immediately, he wanted to know how I got money and who I got it with. This nigga was on some bullshit. Now that Rah has put some hot shit in his ass, it's beef. I'm not ready to choose between my wife and my brother. As a matter of fact, I'm not about to choose.

Since Rahmeek popped Marlo's ass, Niyah has been acting like a real bitch towards me. I have been trying my best to deal with it because I know that she loves her brother. However, I will not deal with her blatant disrespect for me as a man. Niyah has always had a smart ass mouth. That was one of the things I loved about her. She has always known how far to go with me. Since her brother moved in with us, she has no respect for me or this marriage. It's like she trying to show her brother that she's running shit. Niyah is in for a rude ass awakening if she thinks that I'm about to play this game with her.

I had been putting long hours in at the club Just so I could stay away from Niyah's ass. I've noticed that she has been drinking and smoking with her brother. I don't have issue with her drinking and smoking. My issue is that she does it in front of my kids. I had a bad feeling inside of me so I headed home to see if everything was cool. I pulled into my driveway and there were a bunch of other cars parked that I had never seen before. I entered my house and saw wall-to-wall niggas. I was livid. The worst thing a woman could ever do was let random niggas know where her nigga lays his head. Niyah knows better than to be doing shit like this. I searched the house and found Niyah upstairs in the bedroom with our kids. This bitch was watching TV like there wasn't a fucking gang meeting in our living room.

"Who the fuck are all them niggas in my shit!"

"Hey to you too. Those are some my brother's friends."

Niyah was so fucking nonchalant about the situation. I blanked out and yoked her ass up by the collar of her shirt.

"You got less than five minutes to get them niggas and your bitch ass brother out my motherfucking house or it's gon' be a massacre in this bitch!"

"Let me go, Hassan! This is my house too. You just want me to put him out because him and Rahmeek into it.

"Cut the bullshit, Niyah. You know better than to have random niggas in the house where we lay our heads. My motherfucking kids are in here. You know that ain't how we get down, Niyah. We've been in too much shit to be getting reckless right now."

"They're cool, Hassan. You're tripping over nothing. I'm not about to tell my brother to leave my house. Where the fuck will he go?"

"I don't give a fuck where that bitch ass nigga go. As a matter of fact, I see where this shit headed. Since its obvious that your brother means more to you than our safety and well being, I'm leaving. You and your broke ass brother can have this house. I'm taking my kids with me to my OG crib."

Niyah looking in my face and feeling like nothing was wrong with them niggas being in our crib has made me look at her in a totally different light. I have trusted Niyah with my life, but right now, she's looking suspect to me. I grabbed the kids off of the bed and attempted to leave.

"Oh hell no! You're not taking my kids anywhere!" Niyah kept trying to grab Hassan Jr. and Hadiyah.

"Bitch, get the fuck back! I'm not fucking playing with you. Lately, your ass has forgotten who the fuck I am. I'm the same nigga that made an honest fucking woman out you when you weren't shit but a thot. I looked over all that shit because I knew you were riding for me. I'm that same nigga that took you from the hood and got your ass living the lavish lifestyle. You have never had to work or even lift a fucking finger. I make the dough and you spend it. No fucking questions asked. You have had the best of everything. Bitch, I'm the one got you rocking Red Bottoms when I met your ass you were a Air Force One type of chick. Now you standing here saying fuck your husband!"

"I never said fuck you, Hassan." Now she wants to cry these crocodile ass tears.

"Yeah, you said fuck me when you went against what I told you to do. I have never disrespected you or cheated on you, but for you to put me and my kids life in danger has me looking at you differently. I'll be at my OG crib. Come and get them when you get them niggas out the crib."

As I left the house, I locked eyes with Marlo and this nigga had a smirk on his face. This nigga thinks this shit a game. He got me fucked up. I'm not new to this shit. I'm true to this shit. It's definitely about to be some real gunplay if this nigga thinks shit is sweet. My kids being here right now is the only thing keeping me from letting my trigger finger do the talking. Niyah might as well get ready to pick out a casket and a plot. Marlo's ass will not make it to see another year on this Earth.

Chapter 19-Niyah

It hurt me to the core to tell my brother he had to leave my house. I had no other choice. In my heart, I knew that Marlo had been up to no good. I wanted to give him the benefit of the doubt that he could change. At first, I was going to go against my husband wishes and allow Marlo to stay. Once Hassan left the house with our kids, I went downstairs to talk to Marlo. I stopped in my tracks when I overheard him talking. He was saying how much he hated Hassan and how he was going to rob and him and his brother. One of his friends asked about me and he simply said, "Fuck her she can get it too."

He spoke with such hatred in his heart. It felt like someone had ripped my heart out of my chest. All I tried to do was be a good sister to him. I opened my home up to him, bought him new clothes, a car, and gave him ten thousand dollars of my husband's hard-earned money to get on his feet. Knowing that he felt that way about me hurt to the core. I gathered myself and told everyone to leave including him. He tried to sit there and act like he was so hurt, but I knew better. His eyes were cold and evil. The old Marlo was back in full effect. All I could do was pray that he wouldn't get killed. That all changed when I went and checked our safe. Fifty grand was missing and I knew he had signed his death certificate. There wasn't a doubt in my mind that Hassan was going to kill him. Hassan is going to kill my ass when he finds out he stole from us because I had no business telling him about our safe anyway.

****

I sat in Ameenah's driveway for about thirty minutes before I gathered the courage to get out and knock. It was raining cats and dogs. I got drenched just running from the car to her door. It was a little after midnight. I had been calling Hassan's phone, but he wasn't answering. His

Benz was in the driveway so I knew that he was here. I rang the bell a couple of times, but no one came to the door. I started to knock and finally Ammenah opened up the door for me. Ammenah stepped to the side and let me in.

"I'm sorry for waking you up."

"It's okay Niyah. Take those wet clothes off and put on something dry. You might as well stay the night. There's a tornado watch and you don't need to be out driving in it. Hassan and the kids are upstairs asleep."

I went up to the guest bathroom and peeled myself out of my wet clothes. I found one of Hassan's tank tops and a pair of his boxers to put on. Hassan and the kids were sleeping when I walked into the guest bedroom. They were both sleeping on his chest. I crawled into bed and snuggled up with them. I laid there in deep thought. Hassan and my kids were the only thing that mattered in this world. My life would be absolutely nothing without them in it. There is no one in this world worth me jeopardizing my family. Not even my brother.

Hassan got up from the bed and took the kids to their own rooms. I laid there staring at the ceiling because I could tell he was still angry with me. The things he said to me really hurt my feelings. Hassan basically told me I wasn't nothing without him. Hassan brought my confidence down a couple of notches when he called me a hoe. I wanted to believe he said it out of anger, but that's how he really felt about me.

"Them niggas still at my motherfucking house?" I looked up and Hassan was standing in the doorway of the room.

"No. I told Marlo to leave. You don't have to worry about him being in your house anymore."

"Why the fuck are you here, Niyah?" Hassan sat on the edge of the bed and fired up a blunt.

"I came over here to bring my family back home and to apologize. I wanted to say I was sorry for not listening to you when it came down to my brother. Everything you said about him was true. Please forgive me, Hassan.

"I don't even think I can trust you anymore. How could I ever forgive you?" He casually puffed on his blunt and I stood in front of him.

"I can't believe that you would even fix your mouth to say something like that. I'll be the first to admit that I was wrong for letting my brother come to our home and cause confusion in our family. However, I'm not sorry for loving my brother. Rahmeek does a lot of fucked up shit and you stand behind him, right or wrong. I have never in my life asked you to choose Rahmeek over me. I have a right to love my brother just like everybody else does."

"I never said you couldn't love his ass. I wanted you to stop playing blind to the fact that he was on bullshit with me and staying in my crib. You know I don't play that disloyal shit. So, let me ask you this. Where the fuck does your loyalty lie in this marriage? The last thing I need is to be sleeping with the enemy."

"If you have to ask where my loyalty lies, it's obvious you don't trust me. Without trust, a marriage is nothing. I'll start looking for somewhere else to stay. It's time I get out and take care of myself. Especially since I'm nothing without you. Thanks for making an honest woman out of me. I guess you felt the need to change me since I was a hoe when you met me."

"Don't try to turn this shit around, Niyah. You know damn well I didn't mean that shit."

"That doesn't make it hurt any less. I have always been a good wife and mother. It hurts to know you feel that way about me. It's all good though."

I walked out of the room and went inside the room with my kids. As soon as he went to sleep, I was getting the hell out of here with my kids.

Chapter 20-Marlo

I love my sister to death and appreciate everything she has ever done for me. She held a nigga down during my entire bid. However, knowing that she chose her husband over me has me hating her ass with a passion. When I first met Hassan, I knew the nigga thought he was the shit. He turned his nose up as soon as I entered their house. At that very moment, I knew I was going to rob and kill his ass. I didn't care that it would hurt my sister or my niece and nephew.

Once I met the nigga that stole Aja that made the plot even sweeter. This nigga, Rahmeek, was even more arrogant than his brother. He ice grilled me as soon as Niyah introduced us. Knowing that he fucked with Markese, Killa, and Boogie's bitch asses made me hate them even more. Back in the day, I made good ass money with them, but they were on some laid-back type shit. That wasn't my style and it still isn't. I like to be in the hood holding court and letting niggas feel my wrath. They thought they were too good to stand on the blocks. Our difference of opinion is what caused us to sever ties. Now years later, they're still on that lame ass shit.

Once Aja kissed me back, I knew it would be easy to get up in them guts. I just knew I had the bitch back wrapped around finger. That wasn't the case though. Rahmeek got a hold on her ass stronger than I ever had. So I'm at her ass too. It's her fucking fault I'm walking on a cane with two damn gunshots to the legs. I can't believe that nigga really shot me over some pussy. His bitch ass should have killed me because I'm at him and anything remotely close to him.

Niyah told me that I had to leave her house because it was causing too many problems in her marriage. I left without argument. I wasn't about to give the nigga Hassan the impression that I needed him or my sister for a place to lay my head. The entire time I had been living in their house I had been stealing from their safe. Niyah really trusted me with a lot of their personal information. The moment she told me where their safe was I found it and cracked the code. I had took over fifty thousand dollars from their ass. Fuck them. The way they spent money, I knew that they weren't going to miss the shit anyway.

While visiting my parole officer, I bumped into a bad ass bitch. She was visiting her parole officer as well. I have been spending a lot of time with her. She is just what I needed to get my mind off of Aja. I still find it hard to believe that she is married with a baby. I envy that because had I not fucked up with her back in the day she would be my wife and the mother of my children. Hopefully, I can build something with my new bitch. I love the fact that she's real down ass bitch. We haven't known each other that long but she does whatever I tell her no questions asked. It doesn't bother me that she has a daughter. I actually like having the little girl around. I usually don't fuck with bitches that already have kids, but Karima and Brooklyn make me rethink that decision.

***

"Hey baby, I hope you're hungry. I cooked fried chicken and macaroni," Karima said as she came into the living room carrying a tray of food dressed in nothing but red lingerie. That's another thing I love about her; she knows how to please and cater to a nigga.

"That's what up. Thanks, Ma."

"I can't wait until I'm able to go out past ten. Staying in this house it getting old. All we do is smoke and fuck," Karima said as she smoked a blunt.

"Damn, I thought you loved that shit, Ma," I said as I took the blunt from her and pulled off it.

"I do. It's just that I want us to go out and do other things. Like go to the movies or out to dinner. It has been so long since I had a man to call my own."

It felt good to know that she wanted to call me her own. I wasn't in love with her just yet, but she was the type of chick I needed beside me when I took these niggas down.

"I promise as soon as my wounds heal, we'll go out as much as we can. We can even take Brooklyn to that place and we can get her one of them expensive ass dolls made to look like her."

"She would love that and so will I."

Karima stood up and positioned herself in between my legs. She bent down and made a trail of kisses from my mouth down my stomach. She unbuckled my pants. She pulled my dick out and began sucking it. She placed her hands behind her back and made love to my dick with her mouth. I laid my head back and smoked the rest of the blunt as she sucked and slobbed all over my dick. I shot all my seeds straight down her throat. Not long after, we fired up another blunt and she straddled me and rode my dick until we both came. Her pussy and her head game was A1. Whoever her baby daddy is had to be out of his mind to ever stop fucking with her.

Chapter 21- Nisa

I keep telling myself that my son is going to pull through. If he dies, I won't be able to take the pain. It's been a month since I gave birth to my son, Keyon Jenkins Jr. (KJ) and I refuse to leave his side. Killa has been at the hospital with us as well. He wasn't able to catch Remi. That bitch better stay hidden because I have plans on torturing the fuck out of her.

Despite the doctor's expectations of our son surviving twenty-four hours, KJ has made great improvements. He's responding to all the medications and treatments that they have given him. I was so excited when he gained a pound. He's a fighter and gets that from his parents. He's not out of the woods just yet. He's still on a ventilator and a feeding tube. He has to be able to breathe on his own and take formula in order for him to survive. All we could do is pray. I have been so exhausted and tired that the doctor sent me home with strict orders to rest. It felt good to be inside my own house and have Killa there to keep me company.

As soon as I went into my house, I went straight to the nursery. I sat in the custom-made rocking chair and thought about how I couldn't wait to rock KJ to sleep in it.

"What's up, baby? Are you good?" Killa said from the doorway.

"I'm good. I just can't wait to bring the baby here so that he can sleep in his own room." I walked out of the nursery to the bedroom. Killa grabbed me, wrapped his arms around my waist, and held me so tight. It felt good being held in his embrace.

"Don't worry baby. KJ will be home as soon as he gets well. I'm about to go out and grab us some Chinese food. You want to roll with me?"

"I'll chill here until you come back. Stop and get us some movies from the Red Box. We can have a movie night." I kissed him on the lips and he left out. I decided to take a long hot bath and just reflect on my life, my baby, and my past indiscretions that I wasn't too happy about. My mind drifted off to Markese. I haven't spoken to him in a minute. Every since our sexual encounter we have avoided each other like the plague. I really don't look at him in that way, but I miss my friendship with him. I was going to make it my business to stop by the house and visit him and Trish. Now that I think about it, I haven't really spoken to anyone. I really missed the whole crew. I needed to call my girls. I missed them crazy bitches.

Once Killa made it back, we chilled for the rest of the night. It felt just like old times. We enjoyed each other's company. I loved that we were getting back to us. Now all we needed was for KJ to come home and our family would be complete.

Chapter 22-Trish

I was dead set on going to Miami with Yasir, but I chickened out. I didn't have the heart to just go out of state with a man I barely knew. Running to another man is not the option to fix my heart. That will only complicate things even more for me. Plus, Lil Markese didn't need to be around another man. I know that Markese would never have my son around another woman. I would just deal with this shit the best way that I could.

Unbeknownst to anyone, I had been following Carmen around for the last two weeks. I couldn't wait for Markese to handle the situation. I had to sit back and put all of this shit into perspective. From the beginning, I have let Markese handle shit. I fell back and I was the obedient wife. That's why this shit has gotten out of control. Carmen sees me as a weak bitch, therefore she has never respected me. I was supposed to get at that bitch from the jump. Instead, I whooped her ass only to turn around and try to kill myself. That was the weakest shit I ever could have done as a woman. If anything, I was suppose to try to kill him and that bitch. Markese was never properly punished for his indiscretion.

The moment I saw him walking hand in hand with that bitch and her kids I was supposed to be done with his ass. I decided to forgive him, I stayed, and we exchanged vows. For better or for worse. Shit is far worse than I ever thought it could be. I'm sick of sitting back and playing these games with Carmen and Markese. Both of these motherfuckers gon' learn today.

I dropped my baby off at Momma Gail's. I smoked a blunt as I sat outside Carmen's house. I knew she was inside; I was just waiting for her to go to sleep. She always cut the lights off at twelve midnight or so. I was glad I found his keys to her house. I knew that he had a set of keys to her house. At one point, he was trying to sell it. I found them in a lockbox he thought I didn't have the combination to.

I jumped out of the car and tightened the hood on my jacket. I patted my pocket to make sure my gun was in place. I made my way up to her door and inserted the key in the lock. The door opened and the inside of the house was pitch black. I heard the TV playing upstairs. I walked up the stairs and found her bedroom. For a bitch who had done so much to hurt others, she was real comfortable and sleeping peacefully.

"Wake up, bitch!"

I slapped her so hard across the face that bitch jumped up and started swinging. I drop kicked the bitch in the midsection and she fell back on the bed and doubled over in pain. I instantly took my gun out and aimed it at her ass.

"Oh shit now! Big bad Trish has show up and showed out." Carmen was clapping and laughing at the same time. This bitch was nuttier than a fruitcake.

"Shut the fuck up and sit down before I kill your ass now instead of later." Carmen was dead ass wrong if she thought she was going to die on her terms. I was running this show and I was going to kill her ass as I saw fit.

"Girl bye. Stop it with the dramatics. Let's get this shit over with, bitch. I don't have shit to live for. You have my man and our kids. I gave him full custody. You should be thanking me. Go ahead, Trish take my life. Please take me out of my misery. You failed the first time and I'm quite sure your weak ass will miss again. How does it feel to have my family, Trish? Yeah, you finally gave Markese a son, but I gave him his first-born son and daughter. Bitch, that trumps your little baby. Have a seat. Let's talk about why you're really here."

"We're way past the talking stage, Carmen."

I emptied my clip in that bitch. I watched as her body fell limp back on the bed. I watched as she suffered and gasped for air. I wasn't quite finished just yet. I took the lighter from my pocket and set the curtains on fire. The room became engulfed in flames. From the doorway, I watched as that bitch struggled to breathe not only from her bullet wounds, but from the smoke. I wanted that bitch to burn up and suffer for all the pain she caused not only me, but my fucking family. I ran out of the house.

I sat back in my car and fired up another blunt as I watched her entire house go up in smoke. I felt so vindicated as I started my car up and drove away. *Checkmate Bitch!*

I drove around aimlessly until I found myself sitting outside of Markese's house. I wanted to talk to him about our marriage and the crime I had just committed. I knew he was going to be mad that I offed Carmen but he would have to deal with it. I tried calling him, but there was no answer. I knew he was there because his car was parked in the driveway. After debating for about thirty minutes, I decided to drive off. As soon as I got ready to turn on the ignition, his door opened up and he walked out, but he wasn't alone. He was with the same chick he was with at the club. My heart sank as I watched their interaction. They were hand in hand. I was crying because I was hurt and mad. My emotions got the best of me and I was out of the car walking towards them.

"So, ya'll a couple now?" I asked as I stood in front of them, blocking them from walking to his car.

"Trish, move out the way. I don't have time for the bullshit. You have no right to ask me any questions about my personal life. You wanted out of this shit, right? Not to mention you've been keeping company with that nigga. So take your ass home and stop embarrassing yourself."

"I'm not embarrassing myself. I suggest you get rid of this bitch because I need to talk to you."

The bitch was getting ready to say something, but Markese gave her that look that said *don't say shit*. I prayed she said something I was ready to knock the fuck out of her. Didn't I tell this half-breed trick that he was my husband?

"Well, right now is not a good time. Come back tomorrow and we can talk," he said as he pulled her back inside the house and slammed the door. I stood there for a minute trying to get over the fact that he just talked to me the way he did. I wanted to bust every window out of his car. That would only cause more chaos. I got back in my car and went straight to the crib . I made sure I got rid of the gun I killed Carmen with. As soon as I pulled into my driveway, a text came through my phone from Yasir.

What you doing Ma?

Nothing getting ready for bed.

Do you want some company?

Yeah. I would love for you to come over.

Any other time I would have never even allowed Yasir inside of my house out of fear that Markese would come over, but he hasn't stepped in the house since the day he left. Plus, he was laid up with that bitch anyway. I needed to be held and made love to in a way that Markese hadn't. I jumped in the shower and waited for Yasir to arrive. I left the door open for him so that I wouldn't have to go downstairs and open it when he arrived. I laid in bed, naked, waiting for him to arrive.

In the midst of trying, to wait up for him I fell asleep. The feeling of someone rubbing their hands up and down my legs jarred me from my sleep. I woke up and Yasir was under the cover making his way towards my pussy. He licked all the way from my feet to the opening of my pussy.

The feeling of his wet tongue on my body made me shiver and get goose bumps all over my body. His tongue game was electrifying.

"Oh shit ,Yasir. That shit feels so good. Please don't stop."

I grabbed his hair and ran my fingers through it as he buried his tongue deep within my walls. I couldn't take it anymore. I pulled him up because I wanted to feel him inside of me.

"You taste so good, Trish." Yasir said as he positioned himself in between my legs. I reached up and kissed him tasting all of my juices.

Yasir took the head of his dick and moved it up and down my opening until I became soaking wet. He inserted himself inside of me and we became as one as he began to make slow and sensual strokes. I swear I felt every inch of him inside of me. He was hitting all the right spots. I had my eyes closed and my head all the way back as I moaned out in pleasure. The clicking sound of a gun caused both of us to stop in midstroke. Yasir jumped up before he could react. Markese, Boogie, Rahmeek, Killa, and Hassan were beating the shit out of him. All I could do was cry and beg for them to stop. This shit was my fault. I would never be able to forgive myself if they killed him.

"Please stop before you kill him!"

I had pulled the covers up over my body and was standing in the corner screaming and hollering begging for them to stop. There was blood all over the walls and the bed. Yasir was kind of big so he wasn't going out without a fight. He was trying his best to fight back, but he was no match for these psychotic motherfuckers. After what seemed like an eternity Yasir finally stopped fighting and moving for that matter. His face was unrecognizable. I cringed at the sight of his eye hanging out of the socket. I knew he was dead. All I could do was sit in the corner of the bedroom and sob. I felt totally responsible for his death. I watched as Killa, Hassan,

Rahmeek, and Boogie dragged Yasir's naked body out of the room. Markese was out of breath and looking at me. I knew he was coming for my ass next. I tried to run out of the room, but Markese caught me by my hair and slammed my ass on the floor with so much force that all the air was knocked out my lungs.

"Really bitch! You the love that nigga that much you're fucking him in my bed and pleading for his fucking life! Regardless of anything I have ever done to you, I have never violated our home by fucking another bitch in it! You call yourself getting you some revenge?"

I was in so much pain I couldn't even respond. I knew at any moment he was about to rain blows down on me.

"I want you out of my motherfucking house. I already got my son from my momma's house since you insist on dropping him off with her and my father every chance you get. Now I know why. So you can be a hoe!"

Markese got up and left my ass on the floor. I balled up in a fetal position and I cried. I don't know how long I laid on the floor. I was too damn scared to move out of fear that Markese was somewhere lurking to lay hands on my ass. I finally gathered the courage to get up and went into the guest room and lay across the bed. I could hear Markese talking to the rest of the crew. I would just leave when I knew he was gone. I was ashamed and embarrassed. I couldn't face him or the crew. I wonder what the fuck they did with Yasir's body that fast.

The next morning I woke up and the previous nights events came back to my mind. I sat up on the side of the bed for a minute before I walked out of the room. I was scared to look inside my bedroom because it was so damn bloody. I peeped in and it was spotless. It looked as if nothing had ever happened. I must have really been sleeping because I heard nothing. I was wrapped up in the same sheet I had the previous night. I looked out of the window and Yasir's car was gone. I hoped that they had let him go, but in my heart, I knew that he was sleeping with the fishes. I heard the kids downstairs in the kitchen. I became scared because I wasn't ready to face Markese. I jumped in the shower and the water felt so good as it hit my body. I placed my head under the water and cried. After letting it all out, I dried myself and threw on a pair of jeans and a t-shirt along with a pair of wheat Timberlands. Markese wanted me out of the house and I wasn't about to fight to stay. I packed as much as I could.

When I went downstairs, Markese was sitting on the couch with his head in hands. That meant he was still upset and I needed to hurry up and get the fuck out of dodge.

"Hey Mommy!" Gabriella and Juan said as they wrapped their arms around my waist. Lil Markese ran towards me as well. I picked him up and kissed him all over his face.

"Hey, my babies." I hugged and kissed them. I looked over at Markese and we made eye contact. It looked like he had been crying.

"Where are you going, Mommy? Can we go with you?"

"Let me talk to Daddy first. Take your brother and ya'll go to the movie room and watch Frozen. I'll be in there in a minute."

Gabriella did as she was told and I watched them to make sure that were completely out of earshot. Lately, they have seen so much drama. The last thing I wanted them to know is that their father caught their mother fucking another man.

I sat down on the couch next to Markese. There were many things I wanted to say, but the words wouldn't come out.

"Thug was gunned down last night." He said as he laid his back on the couch. That's when I saw fresh tears falling down his face. He and Thug were really close so I knew this had fucked Markese all up.

"Oh my God! What the fuck happened?"

"He was shot outside the club. Niggas shot him in front of his fucking wife and mother. That was some bitch ass shit to do. He has four shorties at home that need him. I can't believe my fucking nigga is gone."

I was now crying because I felt so sorry. Thug is the glue that held their family together. I know Tahari is going through it. She and Thug have that type of love that bitches wish for. I needed to get over to her house and console her. We had become so close since we were introduced last year. I grabbed my keys from the coffee table and was ready to head out the door.

"Where the fuck do you think you're going?" Markese roared.

"I was going to go over and sit with Tahari and the kids."

"You can call her on the phone. I want you to get the kids some clothes and take them to the condo. Go straight there. Don't go anywhere without me knowing. Shit is about to get real out here behind this shit. Plus, I'm not too trusting of you and the fucking company you keep."

Markese walked right past my ass out of the door. I wanted to say something back to his ass, but I knew that he was upset. I packed the kids up and we all headed over to his condo. As I drove, all I could think about is all the events that had taken place in a matter of twenty-four hours. Markese was trying to avoid me, but I really needed to talk to him about Carmen before he heard about her death.

Chapter 23- Markese

It's one thing to know that your wife is fucking with a nigga, but it's a whole different story when you see the shit with your own eyes. No matter what I have done to Trish, I would never violate the house that we have built together by bringing a bitch there. I just keep seeing that nigga fucking my wife. The look on her face let me know she was enjoying that shit. Accompanied with the fact that my fucking cousin was just murked made me lose my cool. My emotions got the best of me and I started beating the fuck out of that nigga and my crew followed suit.

The ultimate disrespect came when this bitch was in the corner begging and pleading for this nigga's life. It took everything inside of me not to beat the shit out of her ass. I wanted to kill her ass, but I couldn't kill the mother of my child. Her little boyfriend wasn't so lucky. He was in the wrong fucking place at the wrong fucking time.

When Trish showed up at my condo unexpectedly, I was actually getting ready to take Nadia home. Nadia and I were not a couple. I had only had sex with her once and that was the night of the grand opening. Nadia wanted more than I was willing to give her. I wanted to fix things with my marriage. I told Nadia that it was best she moved on because there was no future for us.

Trish showing up like that and demanding that I talk to her had really pissed me off. Who the fuck did Trish think she was? she no longer wanted to be in a relationship, Not me. I tried on several occasions to fix our shit. She had even got to a point where she was trying to keep my son away from me. I left it alone and fell back. I agreed with the shit because I knew she had become overwhelmed with the Carmen situation. Trish was hurting and she was no longer happy being with me. What the fuck did she want me to do?

She wanted her space so I gave it to her. We both found comfort in other people. The only difference was I never had my son around Nadia and we never fucked in the house we shared. this bitch had my seed around this nigga. I spent my hard earned money building her that dream house. I don't give a fuck what nobody thinks. That bitch violated the code by bringing that nigga in my shit. It doesn't matter if we were separated. I don't play no disrespectful ass shit like that. Her ass is lucky she's still breathing. If Trish knows what's good for her she will tread lightly around me.

The city temporarily closed the club due to the ongoing shooting investigation. With us having criminal backgrounds and being known drug dealers, the police pulled all type of stunts to get our licenses revoked. We all had our ears to the streets trying to figure out who had hit Thug up. Malik and Sarge were quite sure it came from the Italians, but I wasn't too trusting of that theory. The Italians would not have waited until he was coming out of a fucking nightclub. If they wanted to get at him, they would have run up in the crib and killed the entire family including the kids. That's just how they got down.

The events that had transpired over the last twenty four hours had a nigga exhausted. All I wanted to do was go to the crib and go to bed. I pulled into my driveway and I sat there for about an hour before going inside. I smoked a blunt and drank the last of the Remy I had left over from a fifth I had grabbed earlier with Malik. I needed to be tipsy if I had to be around Trish's ass. I have so much anger and frustration inside of me I might end up killing her bitch ass.

My phone was constantly beeping alerting me that I had voicemails. I hadn't been answering any of my phone calls because I was mourning with my family. As if I didn't have enough problems, the first damn voicemail I heard added to the never ending bullshit.

Mr. Jackson, this is Detective Santo and it's imperative that we speak. I'm not sure if you are aware, but a property in which you own in Wicker Park was burned down yesterday evening. We have reason to believe that this was arson. The body of a unidentified woman was found burned beyond recognition. There is now a pending homicide investigation. The body has been transferred over to the Cook County Medical Examiner's Office for autopsy. We need to speak in person ASAP. My number is 773-888-8000. If you don't come in voluntarily, we will come to you.

I became so angry about the message that I began to bang my fists against the steering wheel. This was the last fucking thing I needed. The police are about to be all up in my shit. I was definitely going down to the station to talk to his ass with my lawyer.

I immediately hit up my lawyer and made plans to go in and talk to the detective the following day. It was about three in the morning when I finally walked into the crib. I entered my bedroom and Trish was laying on her stomach in a white lace panty and bra set. She looked sexy as fuck to me. I rocked up just looking at her fat ass sitting up real nice and pretty. Her cheeks were hanging out the bottom.

Temptation was a bitch. However, I wasn't ready to even touch her, let alone make love to her. I immediately took a long cold shower. Once I was finished, I stepped out of the bathroom and Trish was sitting up in bed. She was biting her bottom lip so I knew she had something she wanted to say. I didn't want to hear shit she had to say. I threw on a pair of boxers and laid down in the bed and turned my back to her.

"Markese, I need to talk to you about something."

"I'm not in the mood to talk right now. So lay your ass back down and go to sleep!"

"I killed Carmen."

"What the fuck did you just say?"

I had sat up in bed and was now facing her and she wouldn't make eye contact with me. I had to roughly pull her face towards me so that she could look me in my face. Tears were streaming down her face at this point.

"I killed Carmen," she repeated as she yanked her face out of my hands.

"Why would you do some shit like that without hollering at me first? Do you have any fucking idea what you have done?" Before I knew it, I had slapped the shit out of her.

"Motherfucker! Don't put your hands on me!"

Trish had punched me in my nose causing my shit to leak instantly. I was bent over holding my nose when she punched my ass in my eye. Before I could even counter she was raining down blows on my ass. I fell back on the bed and that's when she straddled me and had her hot pink nine millimeter pointing at my ass. This bitch had lost her mind.

"We've been together for damn near seventeen years. I have put up with the bitches, the disrespect, and the abuse. What you won't do is put your fucking hands on me because I killed that psychotic ass bitch. How dare you question why I murked a bitch? That hoe has made my life a living fucking hell. I pray that bitch suffered as I burned her ass alive. You should have murked that bitch immediately, but since you was playing in your ass, I handled it like the down ass bitch I am. I did what the fuck I had to do to protect me and my family. I don't want to hear shit else about the bitch. Do you understand, Markese?

"You better get that fucking gun out of my face," I said through gritted teeth.

She cocked back the hammer as she spoke. "I said, do you understand?"

"Yeah. I understand." I was mad as hell but the look in her eyes let me know I better answer or else she would blow my fucking brains out.

"While you're running around here mad and pissed off because I'm fucking somebody else, Let's talk about you and that bitch you've been parading around the city. Do I have to pay a visit to that bitch's house? I'm on a roll and I'm killing any bitch I think will cause a problem in my life or my fucking marriage. Hopefully, that shit is a dead ass issue. For that bitch's sake, she need to move on and count whatever the fuck ya'll had going as a loss. If not, she will meet the same fate as Yasir. It's only right I get to murk that bitch since you killed him."

I couldn't believe that Trish ass was holding me at gunpoint and throwing out demands and shit. At first I was scared, but now that shit had my dick harder than a motherfucker. That was until she said some shit that threw me for the loop.

"I have one more question for you. Have you ever fucked Nisa?"

"What? Get the fuck out of here. You know that's my sister. Why would you ask me some shit like that?" I was trying my best to keep a straight face and a serious tone. Trish's ass has a way of deciphering shit.

"I knew you were going to say that. I'm not trying to hear that sister shit. Let's just say you talk in your sleep and I got an ear full. I have been through too much to deal with you fucking someone so close to us. You don't have to worry about me saying anything about this to her or Killa. Don't get it twisted; I will be watching both of ya'll like a fucking hawk. If

I even think ya'll on some bullshit, both of ya'll won't even be ready for what I have in store for ya'll asses."

I really had nothing to say. As soon as Trish uncocked the gun and sat it on the nightstand, I immediately knocked her over and it was my turn to point a gun at her. She might have laid down the law, but I run the motherfucking show.

"Get your black ass off of me!"

I pinned her arms down with my knees because I knew her ass was ready to punch my ass again. My nose was still leaking and my eye was throbbing. If I have a black eye I'm going to be so fucking mad.

"It don't feel so fucking good to have a fucking gun pointed in your face. Does it? The last thing you need to be worried about is if I'm fucking another bitch. I wanted my marriage to work. it was you who wanted out. So I gave your ass an outlet. I'll admit, I was sick behind you fucking dude, but when I saw that shit I had to off his ass. Did you like that shit he was doing to your hoe ass? Yeah, you liked it. I saw it in your face," I said her as I pressed the gun to the middle of her forehead. She didn't respond she just stared at me.

"Cat got your fucking tongue now? Just a minute ago you wouldn't shut the fuck up. I got something that will make your ass talk though."

I ripped her panties off of her with my free hand as I continued to hold the gun to her head. I pulled my dick out my boxers and I made it find its way to her pussy hole. I rammed my entire dick inside of her.

"Ahhhh! I hate your ass!" she yelled as I thrusted in and out of her.

I was trying my best to block out the fact that not too long ago another nigga was in between her legs taking what the fuck belonged to me. That shit made me want to punish her ass even more.

"Oh you hate me now?"

I sped up the pace and mad sure my dick was damn near touching her soul. I roughly flipped her ass over and started hitting her ass from the back. I grabbed her long hair and wrapped it around my hand. I continued to fuck her brains out and that shit had me feeling real powerful because I knew she was loving that shit. Especially when she was running from the dick.

"Where the fuck you going? Take this dick like you was taking that niggas last night."

Her screams were replaced with loud moans. I wanted to moan as well because her pussy felt good as hell. I felt my cum rise to the tip of my dick and released my load inside of her. She collapsed on the bed and I fell on top of her. We were both out of breath and heavily breathing. I heard my son start to cry so I got up to go check on him. I grabbed him from his bed and brought him back into our bedroom. Trish was sitting up in the bed. As I walked back in the room I noticed her wiping her face. She reached out for him and he went to her.

"Markese, we are so selfish and ungrateful," she said as she kissed our son's forehead.

"What the fuck is that supposed to mean?"

"We have money, kids, our health, and most importantly we have each other. I can't believe we just sat here and really had guns pointed at each other. You might not believe me, but I don't know what I would do if you were killed. All I keep thinking about is Tahari and her kids. Thug is gone. I couldn't even imagine living life without you, but I'm fighting you and trying to hurt you. My biggest fear is Tahari's reality. I remember when I couldn't give you a baby and now we share a son. Yet, we sit up and expose him to shit that we shouldn't. We should be enjoying life, not acting like we don't appreciate it. All this bullshit that has been going on has caused both of us to lose sight of what really matters and that's family. The only way we're going to make it is if we let go of all the animosity. That is if you want the shit to work out."

I had to take in everything that Trish was saying and agreed with all of it. The last thing I want is for us to keep fighting like this and exposing our kids to this shit. My childhood was all fucked up, but that's not what I want for my kids. They've been through enough.

"I agree with all that, Trish. I need you to understand that when shit gets rough in this marriage, I need you to stick it out. You're my wife, my better half. when you chose to walk out on a nigga that shit hurt me because I have never turned my back on you when you needed me. We can go on and on about who's right and who's wrong. It won't change shit. It's up to us the fix it. I'm willing to work this shit out, but I don't have time for all this sneaky shit."

I cut the light off and laid down in the bed.

"I want to fix it." She leaned over and gave me a quick peck on the lips

"Good because this the last time I'm letting your crazy ass pull a pistol on me and let you live to tell about the shit."

"Yeah whatever nigga. I bet you got my fucking point."

"Loud and clear."

The next morning I met up with my lawyer and went to talk to the Detective who called me. (Finish this with him at police station)

Chapter 24-Lupe Rodriquez

Since the day that I was deported, I never ever thought of paying a visit to Chicago. That was until I got the news that my one and only child had been murdered. I sent Yasir there to watch over Carmen and kill Markese. Instead, he starts fucking Trish. Now he is missing. It's a damn shame that I have to come all the way to Chicago and handle these motherfuckers myself.

I really hate that Carmen was so fucking weak. One would think I didn't love her, but that wasn't true. I had to treat her the way I did in order for her to become a heartless bitch like me. I knew from the jump, she was cut from a different cloth than me. She was a woman scorned who let her love for a man dictate her life. It was my love for Juan that led me to become a woman scorned. That love also turned my heart to stone. I became so coldhearted that I had no problem with killing anyone with the snap of a finger.

I guess I despised the fact that I was once in her shoes. I had the world at my feet courtesy of my father. He was one of the world's biggest drug traffickers. My father had the purest heroin all over Colombia. Juan was one of my father's workers. My father had no idea that I had been having a sexual relationship with Juan. Juan insisted on telling him that he wanted to marry me. I was scared for his life because my father would not take kindly to Juan fucking me behind his back. Juan was lucky that my father was one of his most loyal workers. My father trusted Juan with his product and eventually with me his only daughter. Our drug trafficking operation began to expand into the states. So, my father sent Juan and I to Chicago. We were in charge of the entire operation. I became pregnant with Carmen, so I stepped back and let Juan run the show. Once I gave birth, I was ready to get back in the swing of things. I ended up hiring Ammenah. A decision that I still regret to this day. As I ride in the back of my Lincoln Towncar my mind drifted back to the day I caught my husband fucking the help.

It was a beautiful Sunday morning. I woke up to the sun shining and the birds chirping. Despite how beautiful it was, I was in a real dark place. I had just received a call from Colombia informing me that my father had a heart attack and died. I was now head of his drug operation. My husband and I were about to be the King and Queen of Heroin.

I walked down the long corridor of our home. Beautiful portraits of our family aligned the walls. I stopped at the poster size picture of my father. "Voy a hacer que te sientas orgulloso de mi padre."

I told him that I would make him proud of me. I kissed his picture and continued down the long corridor. Once I made it to Carmen's bedroom, I opened the door and checked on her. She was sleeping soundly. I continued the search for my husband. I checked his office, but he wasn't there. H wasn't in the kitchen or any other common areas of our home. It was oddly strange that Ammenah was not around either. Since she stayed in the guest house, I proceeded out of the back door and towards the guest house. I didn't even knock I just went straight in. The sounds of moaning caught my attention instantly. I slowly crept towards the bedroom. There was Juan on top of Ammenah. I turned and walked away.

That was the moment I became a heartless bitch. I dished out my revenge slowly, but surely. Juan was a beast when it came to the drug trade. I needed him to keep my operation afloat. I started having an affair with Chico just to get over Juan. However, Ammenah got the brunt of all my anger. Once I found out that she was pregnant, I went full steam ahead in fucking up her very existence.

I took that bitch of a daughter from her away and made her my drug mule. The hatred I harbored in my heart for these women is what led to my deportation. That's why I was disappointed in Carmen. She was better than being a woman scorned. It's too late for regrets now because my daughter is dead. I have a real big problem with these people being alive that hurt her.

Despite being in Mexico, I had eyes and ears all over Chicago. I'm not the Queen for shit. I know names and addresses. I have a long list of people I need to pay a visit. My first stop is Stacy's house . I have something I think that she would like to see. This bitch and her mother are living off of my fucking money. Juan better be happy he's already dead because I want to blow his brains out. He, his mistress, and their love child are still fucking my life up after all these years.

Chapter 25- Stacy

The positive sign on the pregnancy test confirmed what I already knew. I was pregnant with Boogie's baby. I couldn't wait to tell him the good news. The last week had been rough on us all. Thug's funeral had already taken place. It was now time for the healing to start. Boogie had been keeping his promise of not touching heroin anymore. I was so happy and proud of him because I knew how hard it was to shake a dope habit. Our relationship had become stronger than ever. This pregnancy is just what we need to make our bond stronger.

I was preparing dinner for us when the doorbell rang. I turned the burners on the stove down low and rushed to the front door. I swung the door open without answering or looking in the peephole. The person standing on the other side of the door was my worst nightmare come true. I instantly regretted not looking through the peephole.

"Surprised to see me, huh? The last time I saw you we were in court and you were testifying against me." Lupe Rodriquez and her two goons pushed past me and made their way into my home without permission.

"What the fuck do you want, Lupe? If you came here to kill me, let's get this shit over with. I know this isn't a social call so what the fuck do you want."

Lupe walked around my living room and looked at the pictures on my mantle of Boogie and me. Her two goons were positioned by the door.

"You always did have a way with words. By the way, how's that bitch of a mother of yours?"

"My mother is just fine unlike your miserable ass."

She let out a chuckle as she continued to survey my living room. I still couldn't believe this crazy bitch was in my living room.

"I came here to show you something."

One of her goons handed me a large manila envelope. I took it from his hands and opened it. As I thumbed through the pictures, the life drained from inside of me.

"Surprised I know about him, huh? The look on your face tells me your husband has no idea about him."

Tears streamed down my face as I looked at pictures of my son that I gave up for adoption so long ago. I put him in the back of my mind, but I always kept him close to my heart. I've sent him a ten thousand dollar check every month since I came into the money Juan had left for me.

"Please don't hurt him, Lupe. He has nothing to do with any of this mess. I'm the one who you want."

"You really love the little black bastard, huh? I tell you what. I'll spare his life in exchange for ten million dollars. Please don't say you don' have it. I'm fully aware of the inheritance Juan left you. I deserve some type of restitution for all the pain and suffering you have put me through. If you value his life and yours, you'll have my money by week's end. Here is my card; call me when you're ready to talk."

Lupe threw her card on the floor and walked out of the house followed by her goons. I couldn't believe this shit was happening to me. All the pain and suffering this bitch caused me. She wasn't getting a dime from me. As much as I hated to do it, I had to come clean with Boogie about our nine-year-old son, Kendrick Jr.

It had been two days since Lupe's visit. I was so scared and nervous, not to mention the morning sickness had kicked in big time. I decided that today would be the day I told him. I hoped and prayed he understood why I did what I did. I had yet to tell him I was pregnant. I wanted to wait until after he knew about our first-born child. I sat up in our bed and waiting for him to finish his shower. After waiting about twenty minutes, he emerged.

"Why you looking like somebody died?"

I didn't answer him. I got up from the bed and grabbed the pictures Lupe had given me. I handed the pictures to him and sat back down on the bed. I watched as he looked at all of the pictures one by one. There were about ten in all.

"Who the fuck is this?' he asked as he threw the pictures on the bed.

"He's my son-our son," I said as I my words got caught up in my throat.

Boogie was in the process of throwing on a T-shirt and a pair of basketball shorts. He turned around and spoke to me with the meanest scowl on his face. "What the fuck did you just say?"

"I wanted to tell you about him, but I was too scared they would hurt him. When I almost died from transporting the drugs, I found out I was four months pregnant. The doctor refused to give me an abortion because I was too far gone in the pregnancy. Without a doubt in my mind, I knew he was yours. I gave him up for adoption to protect him. I never meant to hurt you. I'm so sorry that I didn't tell you sooner. What was I supposed to do, Boogie? I was a witness for the FEDS and on the run for my life." I was on my knees in front of him trying to explain.

"Get the fuck out!"

"I'm not leaving, Boogie. we need to talk about this shit."

"Bitch, you're getting the fucking out of here!"

Boogie slapped me and I fell to the floor. He grabbed my hair and began dragging me out of our bedroom and down the stairs.

"Please stop! Please stop! Baby, you have to let me explain!"

I cried and pleaded, but it fell on deaf ears. I could feel the hairs on my head being ripped from the roots as he continued to drag me. I fought and I kicked trying to get away from him. He was just too strong for me. Once we got by the door, he flung it open and threw me out on my ass. I tried to hurry up and catch the door before he closed it, but I wasn't quick enough. He threw my purse and a pair of gym shoes out of the window. I was glad I had on a jogging suit. I continued to bang on the door, but he never opened it for me.

I got inside my car and drove to the house that Juan had left for me. I was glad that it was already furnished. Once I made it to the house, I had the urge to pee. After finding a bathroom I sat down to piss and that's when I saw small amounts of blood. I hopped back in the car and drove myself to the hospital. It was then I realized I never told got a chance to tell Boogie I was pregnant. I also needed to tell him about Lupe's visit. That old bitch is up to no good.

After going to the emergency room, the doctor informed me that I was twelve weeks pregnant. He told me to just get some rest. The visit from Lupe had my nerves all rattled. I was so worried about my mother. I needed to talk to someone about what was going on. I was scared to call my brothers because they would know about my son. I needed my girls to help me. Right about now, they're my last hope. I was not about to pay Lupe shit. I would kill that bitch dead before I let her ruin my family. I've worked hard to rebuild my life. She will not come in and tear down everything that I have built.

****

"This house is huge. I can't believe you and Boogie have not moved in here," Aja said as turned over the chicken she was frying.

"Boogie refuses to step one foot inside of this house."

"Since we're on the subject of your husband, what's going on with ya'll? Why are you living here and he's living in the other house?"

"It's a long story and I don't feel like telling it twice. As soon as the girls get here, I'll tell you everything."

Trish, Niyah, and Nisa finally arrived. We sat around the dining room table eating fried chicken and spaghetti. The aura in the room was all off. I could tell I wasn't the only one who had shit going on in my life.

"I'm glad you guys came on such a short notice. I really need your help. I don't know what I'm going to do." I became so upset I was shaking.

"What's wrong?" Niyah asked as she got up from her seat and sat next to me.

"Do you guys remember when I told everyone about being a drug mule for Lupe?"

"Yeah, we remember." Nisa said and all of the girls agree in unison.

"I left out a very important piece of the puzzle. When I was rushed to the hospital and the drugs were removed I was informed that I was pregnant. I knew that I was pregnant by Boogie because I had never been with anyone else. I was too far along, so I couldn't get an abortion. I carried the baby full term. Once I gave birth to him I gave him up for adoption to a really good friend of mine. I couldn't tell Boogie about the baby. He would have made me come back to Chicago. I couldn't risk me or my son's life like that. Life has been going good for me. That was until Lupe showed her crazy ass up at my door. She has pictures of my son and says she wants ten million dollars in exchange for his life. I had no other choice but to come clean and tell Boogie the truth.

As I told the girls what had happened, all I kept seeing in my head was my son and the look on Boogie's face when I told him about our son. I was crying a river at this point.

"What did Boogie say?" Nisa asked as she held my hand.

"He told me to get the fuck out. I refused so he dragged me out. He was so angry with me. I never even got a chance to tell him about Lupe or that I'm pregnant."

"Awwww, I'm going to be an auntie," Aja said and she started rubbing my stomach. All the girls did the same.

"I need your help. We have to get rid of that bitch. I know how she operates. There is more to her being here in Chicago. She didn't come all the way to Chicago to extort me. She has more money than she knows what to do with."

"She's here because Carmen is dead," Trish said as a devilish grin crept across her face.

"Hold the fuck on! That bitch is dead and I didn't get a chance to shoot the bitch first. Who killed her ass?" Nisa asked as she got up and banged on the table.

"I did. Stacy, do you have any liquor around here?" Trish was acting as if she had not just dropped a damn bombshell on us.

"There's a wine cellar straight through the kitchen. I have never been down there. So I'm not sure if there is anything down there."

"Does Markese know that you did it?" Aja asked with a worried look on her face.

"Yeah, he knows. That bitch Carmen is dead. Now we have to kill the bitch who gave birth to her. I'm sick and tired of people hurting this family. We've worked too hard to keep going through these changes. I'm killing any and everything that fucks with me, my family, and my husband."

Trish looked Nisa in her eyes as she put emphasis on the husband part. I hope Nisa caught on because I got the message. We all speculated at one time or another about the relationship between Nisa and Markese. I guess Trish has her suspicions as well. Trish walked out of the room and went to the wine cellar. The room was quiet as we all sat and tried to take in everything that had been said. Trish came back upstairs empty handed looking as if she had seen a ghost.

"What the fuck is wrong with you?" I asked as she sat down at the table.

"I think ya'll need to go downstairs and look at what's down there."

"I hope ya'll ain't got me in this house and it's a damn dead body down there." Niyah said as we all got up minus Trish and went downstairs. As soon as I entered the cellar, I felt as if I would pass out. There were kilos everywhere, Lined up neatly against the walls. I saw a door and opened it and there were more kilos. I had to take a seat on the steps to keep from fainting.

"Oh my God. It's snowing in this motherfucker!" Nisa said as she ran her hands all over the neatly wrapped kilos that were packaged in clear plastic. "Look, there's an envelope with your name on it." Nisa handed me the letter that was attached to one of the bricks. I slowly opened it and I began to read it.

My Mija,

If you're reading this letter, you have found my hidden treasure. The enclosed map will show you where you can find the rest of my heroin, which you now own. My empire is now yours. I hope that you have got in contact with your brothers and their crew. They will know what to do with it all. I know there is nothing I can say or do that will change what happened to you. I hope in time you forgive me.

Juan

"What are you going to do with all this shit, Stacy?" Aja asked as she sat on the stairs next to me.

"I guess I need to call our husbands. I wouldn't know what to do with all this shit. I retired from the drug game a long ass time ago."

I handed the letter to them so that they could read it. I stood up and tried to call Boogie, but he hung up in my face. He made sure to tell me not to call his phone anymore. I had no other choice but to call Rahmeek and Hassan. It's too much shit going on in my life right now.

Chapter 26- Rahmeek

It had been about a month since I saw my daughter, Brooklyn. The first couple of weeks after Karima was released she brought Brooklyn over on the weekends like clockwork. Lately, Karima has been MIA. I stopped showing up at Karima's house unannounced, but since she is not answering the phone, I don't have a choice. Some shit is not sitting right with me. Karima has no reason to keep Brooklyn away from me and Aja. My mother has even tried on several occasions to get in contact with her. Karima better hope my daughter is okay. I swear I'm going to put a bullet in her fucking head. If she values her life there won't be a hair out of place on my daughter's head.

I scooped up Hassan to ride with me over to Karima's crib. Once we arrived I let myself in with my key, but they weren't there. The house was in good condition with the exception of previously smoked Black and Milds in the ashtray. Karima didn't smoke shit but weed. That meant she probably was fucking with some nigga that did smoke them. She couldn't keep any friends because she was too scandalous so they definitely didn't belong to a woman.

Hassan and I went back out to the car. Curiosity got the best of me and I decided to wait until Karima returned. I pulled out of the driveway and I parked a couple of doors down from her house. I made sure I parked so that I could see a clear view of the front of her house. I wasn't sure how long we would have to wait so I fired up a blunt and got comfortable.

"What's up with you and Niyah?" I asked Hassan as I passed the blunt to him.

"We're good now. It was hell trying to get her to stay after the shit I said to her. I'm just glad she has finally realized that her brother is a damn user. Do you know that nigga was stealing from my fucking safe? Over fifty thousand gone. I wanted to beat the fuck out of Niyah for being so damn stupid. Once she realized the money was missing, she had to come clean. She told him about the safe. I know that's her brother and all, but how could she be so fucking naive. I already told her to get her tears out of the way now because I'm going to kill him."

"We aren't the only ones at his head. Word on the street is he's been robbing Thug's trap houses since his death. We already know Marlo won't make it another month if Malik and Sarge are at his head. I just hope and pray we get to his ass before they do."

Hassan and I continued to chop it up until I received a call from Stacy telling us that she needed us to get over to her house ASAP. I heard the urgency in her voice so I called Markese, Killa, and Boogie. I'm not sure what's going on between him and Stacy, but it has him acting like a real bitch. I hated to leave before catching up with Karima, but I needed to go see what was going on with my sister.

When I walked inside of the house, I didn't know what to think. Every time these woman got together like this they had either done some shit they had no business doing or bullshit was on the horizon. "What the fuck have ya'll done now?"

"We haven't done anything yet," Nisa said as she walked over to Killa and kissed him.

"I know that you're wondering why I called you. There is something in the wine cellar that I need you to see. Before you go down there I need you to know that I had no idea about any of this shit," Stacy said as she led the way to the wine cellar.

"Why do I have a hard time believing that?" Boogie said as he pushed Stacy out of his way.

We continued to follow her downstairs to the cellar. As soon as I stepped inside the wine cellar, I had to blink my eyes a couple of times to make sure my eyes weren't deceiving me.

"Are you sure you had no idea about this shit?" Boogie asked as he surveyed the kilos that were lined up around the room.

"I promise you, we just found it today. I would never hide anything like this from any of you. I know how hard it has been without a connect. I'm down for whatever ya'll decide to do."

"First things first, we need to move all this shit to our warehouse ASAP. I'll go order a large moving truck. We can move the shit ourselves. We can all meet up and discuss if we're back in the drug game or not. I also think it's imperative that our wives join us in this meeting. It's only right they have a say in this shit."

The rest of the crew agreed and we got to work counting the bricks so they could be transported to our warehouse. Stacy slipped a piece of paper in my hand. Once I read it, I knew we were back in the drug game.

****

Everyone had finally arrived at the warehouse and we were all sitting around the conference table. I made sure we had liquor and plenty of blunts. We were all going to need it for the talk we were about to have. I observed everyone sitting around either drinking or smoking. The look on their faces told me that they were all in deep thought. I hated he aura in the room because our meetings have never been quiet. There was always someone who had something to say. In order for us to think about our next move, everyone needed to air their grievances with one another. I knew that I needed to be the one to break the silence.

"So, Stacy what do you want to do with all these bricks?" Stacy fidgeted with her fingers not making eye contact with anyone.

"I'm down for whatever the crew wants to do. That's all of our shit. Plus, the letter that Juan left behind lets me know that there is more where that came from. What do you think, Boogie?"

"Does it really matter what the fuck I think?" Boogie said as he knocked back a shot of Remy. I observed the girls all looking down not making eye contact with any of us. That let me know they knew what was going on between them.

"What the fuck is going on with ya'll?" Hassan asked as he took a long pull from the blunt.

"Let me guess. You didn't tell your brothers about their nephew?"

Stacy looked at Boogie with so much contempt and hurt. He was trying his best to break her down.

"I have been trying my best to stay out of this, but what the fuck does he mean by nephew?"

I didn't mean to upset Stacy. She was already very upset and crying. I was just getting more livid with all these subliminal messages.

"I'm sorry I didn't tell you guys sooner. I have a nine-year-old son by Boogie. I gave him up for adoption because I feared for his life. When I passed out in the airport, I was four months pregnant, but I didn't know until afterwards. I was on the run from Lupe. I couldn't put his life in danger for my fuck-ups. At that time, I never ever thought I would see Boogie again. I have never regretted my decision because he is in good hands. A couple of days ago, Lupe Rodriquez came to our house and showed me pictures of him. She wants me to give her ten million dollars in exchange for his life. That same day I found out I was pregnant. Twelve weeks to be exact."

"Why the fuck you didn't tell me all that shit?" Boogie said as he banged on the table with his fist. Stacy jumped from the booming sound of his voice. Tears fell from her ass soaking the table.

"You were too busy dragging me out the house by my hair."

I had to clench my jaws tight and keep calm. I had never seen my sister so upset. That shit was killing me slowly and I could tell Hassan was also in his feelings. We couldn't react because that's not what Stacy wanted. They needed to get in private and work this shit out. In the meantime, we needed to focus on Lupe Rodriquez and what the hell we were going to do with all the bricks we had on deck.

"If Lupe Rodriquez is here on bullshit that means Carmen is right with her," Killa said as his jaws clenched.

"Carmen is dead. I already offed her ass. Now we just need to focus on killing her psycho ass mother. I'm ready for whatever," Trish said as she knocked back a shot of Patron and pulled her nine from the small of her back. It made the loudest noise as it banged against the table.

We all were shocked at her nonchalant confession. We just looked at her as she fired up a blunt and knocked back shot after shot. I looked over at Markese and his facial expression let me know that Carmen really was dead. All he could do was shake his head and drink straight from the Remy bottle. Trish has been in rare form lately and Markese doesn't know what to do about it.

"I'm tired of sitting around shooting the breeze. Can we please put this plan together? I want to rid my life of all things that's hindering our family's growth. I know ya'll mad I didn't talk to ya'll first, but I was tired of waiting around while that bitch destroyed us. Now her mother is here on some bullshit. Oh hell no! We need to off this old bitch immediately."

"I agree with Trish. She definitely has to go," Nisa said and everyone agreed with her. I was getting ready to respond, but my cell phone rang. I looked at the screen and it read Karima. I quickly answered before she hung up.

"Where the fuck is my daughter?"

Karima was on the other end of the phone and I she sounded like she was crying.

"Brooklyn got shot! Please Rah come to the County Hospital!" What Karima said had to resonate inside my brain. I just held the phone in shock.

"Rahmeek! Rahmeek! Baby, what's wrong?" Aja was yelling and shaking me out my trance.

"We need to get to the hospital. Brooklyn got shot." I rushed out of the warehouse with everyone behind me. As I drove to the hospital, all I could think about was my baby girl. Her first birthday is in two weeks and some wannabe gangsta shot her. I have never been the type of nigga who asked God for anything. At that very moment, I prayed and asked God to heal my daughter. Aja squeezed my hand so tight as we pulled up to the hospital parking lot. We found a park and ran towards the hospital entrance. The entire crew was not far behind us. I walked up to the nurses' station to find out about Brooklyn's status. Before I could get any words out Karima's voice caught my attention. I looked around and saw her and Marlo talking to the police. I lost all of my cool and sanity when I heard him say that he was Brooklyn's father. I was about to kill both of these motherfuckers.

Chapter 27-Karima

The first month or so of dealing with Marlo was pure bliss. We were having so much fun and enjoying ourselves. Once his gunshot wounds healed, all he wanted to do was run the streets and rob niggas. He was bringing home large sums of money splurging it on me and my daughter. Everything was going good until he persuaded me into setting up local drug dealers for him.

At first I was dead set against it but eventually I gave in. Marlo was in my head and I couldn't get him out. I loved the fact that he lived on the edge and had an *I don't give a fuck* attitude. It felt good to finally have a man of my own. I was finally able to go out in public and show the world my new man. We were robbing niggas left and right without any fuckups. We were on some Bonnie and Clyde type of shit.

In such a short time, Marlo managed to pull me in deep. The last thing that was on my mind was Rahmeek. I finally found someone to fill the void Rahmeek left in my heart. I knew if I told him about my new boyfriend, he would act a fool. Rahmeek wants to run every aspect of my life. I think that he forgets that he is Brooklyn's father not mine. Since I was arrested, he thought that I was incompetent. His ass must have forgotten that I took care of my daughter before he even knew she existed. I just decided to keep Brooklyn away from him and Aja until I could figure out how to tell him about Marlo. The last thing I wanted to do was keep Brooklyn from her daddy. However, I knew that Rahmeek would take Brooklyn away from me if he knew I had her around another man.

The shooting happened so fast. We were driving down State Street on our way to go shopping. We stopped at a light and a car stopped alongside us. I was trying to get a good look at the two men inside the car because they were staring. The man in the passenger seat rolled down the window.

I was able to get a good look at him and remembered he was one of the guys I had tricked for Marlo to set up and rob him.

Marlo was engrossed in watching the road he never even paid attention to the car next to us. The car was closer on my side. The driver pulled the gun out so fast that I didn't have to react. He started shooting inside the car. As soon as the light changed, the car sped off. At first Brooklyn was crying from the noise thenall of a sudden she stopped. Marlo was now speeding down the sheet like a speed racer hitting other cars in the process.

"Oh my God, Lo! They shot my baby! Hurry up and get us to the hospital!"

"Calm down we're almost there!" Marlo said as he never took his eyes off the road.

About five minutes later, we pulled right in from of the Emergency entrance Marlo jumped out and snatched Brooklyn from my arms and we ran inside. The doctors immediately rushed her to the back and started working on her. I knew I had to call Rahmeek.

The nurse bought some papers over to me and I filled them out. I sat down in one of the chairs and tried to gather myself. I should have known better than to have Brooklyn riding in a car with us. We had fucked over too many people.

"Are you the parent of Brooklyn Jones?" A plain-clothes detective asked me.

"Yes."

"We need to ask you some questions about what happened."

"I'm Brooklyn's father. You can talk to both of us." I looked at his ass like he was crazy. He gave me that look that said *shut the fuck up and don't say shit.*

Before I could even turn around and finish talking to the detective, Rahmeek came out of nowhere and charged at Marlo. They were fighting and throwing punches at one another.

"Stop that shit!" I was screaming and trying to pull them apart. Out of nowhere, Aja just started hitting me. I wanted to counter but before I could, hospital security and the police broke us up.

"That bitch ass nigga is not her father. That's my daughter!" Rahmeek yelled as he was being held by the police.

"What the hell are you doing here with Karima?" Niyah asked Marlo as he wiped blood from his nose.

"What the fuck you mean? That's my girl and my baby. Why the fuck do you care? Get the fuck away from me, Niyah."

As soon as the words left his mouth I observed Hassan jump up from the seat and charge at Marlo, but Killa and Markese held him back.

"Wait. What the fuck is going on, Marlo? How do ya'll know each other?"

I was confused as hell right now because the couple of months that we've messed around He has never mentioned Niyah.

"Shut your stupid ass up, Karima! This is my brother and you can quit playing the nut roll. Your ass is fully aware of his connection to us."

"I just met Marlo. I had no idea that he knew ya'll. I never mentioned Rahmeek to him either." I was crying uncontrollably trying to wrap my mind around the fact that this nigga had played my ass.

"Bitch, you had my daughter around this nigga!"

Rahmeek was now fighting the police trying to get to me. That made Hassan, Killa, Markese and Boogie join in on the melee, which made their psychotic ass wives jump in the fight too. I couldn't believe they were in this hospital humbugging like this. They were fighting the police and the hospital security. In the midst of them fighting the police, I observed Marlo sneak past everyone and bolt out of the emergency room.

Coward ass nigga!

Once the fight was broken up, they were all arrested and taken out in handcuffs. Rahmeek wasn't arrested due to him being Brooklyn's father. A part of me wanted him to get locked up because I knew he was going to kill me. We were placed in different areas of the waiting area to keep down the confusion. The police questioned me and I told them exactly what happened. About two hours later, the doctors came out to talk with us. I wiped my eyes and ran over to her.

"Please tell me my daughter is going to make it," Rahmeek asked with tears in his eyes. Seeing him so upset made me feel like shit.

"we have her stabilized. She was shot in both of her legs. The injuries were severe. We performed surgery on her legs to repair them. Both of her legs have been casted. She will need extensive therapy when she starts walking. The other injuries that she sustained were graze wounds. They will all heal in time. Little Brooklyn is a very lucky girl. She's in the Pediatric Intensive Care Unit. You can go back there and see her."

"Thank you so much." I said to the doctor as Rahmeek and I made our way back to visit Brooklyn. Once we were inside Brooklyn's room and away from the doctor's and the police. Rahmeek wrapped his hands around my throat and slammed me against the wall.

"If you value your life, you will pack a bag and book a motherfucking flight. Consider your parental rights revoked," Rahmeek said through gritted teeth.

His hands were around my throat were so tight I thought that I would pass out at any minute. He roughly let me go and I fell into the chair alongside Brooklyn's bed. Rahmeek sat with Brooklyn for a minute and I watched as he whispered in her ear and kissed her on the forehead.

"You have less than twenty four hours to disappear," Rahmeek said to me before he exited the room. I sat with my daughter and explained to her why I had to leave. I prayed that she could hear my cries. I placed soft kisses on her forehead and I left.

I rushed home to pack. I was unsure of where I was going. I just knew I needed to get as far away from Marlo and Rahmeek as I could.

"Going somewhere?" Marlo asked as he stood in the doorway of my bedroom.

"I'm getting as far away from your grimy ass as possible. All this shit is your fault. I thought we had something special. All along, you knew who my baby daddy was. It's your fault why my daughter is laying in a fucking hospital bed. Now Rahmeek is taking my daughter from me." I continued to move around the bedroom putting things into my suitcase.

"Fuck that nigga and his motherfucking daughter! Bitch, I know you were setting me up for that nigga! What did you tell him about me?" Marlo had a gun pointed at me.

"Put that gun down, Marlo! I didn't tell him anything about you!" I yelled as I tried to back up away from him.

He had a wild look in his eyes. I tried to run to the door, but he started shooting me. I fell face down on the carpet. The burning sensation from the bullets that entered my body was so painful. I was aware of everything going on in the room. I felt him standing over me and that's when he pressed the gun behind my ear. He pulled the trigger and it was all over for me. Lights out. The life I had never even had a chance to flash before my eyes. Marlo had silenced me forever.

Chapter 28-Boogie

The news of me having a seed out here in the world had really fucked me up in the head. I actually thought that I was shooting blanks. Stacy and I have always had unprotected sex and she doesn't use birth control. I'm so disappointed in her right now. I understand she had things going on in her life, but I had a right to know that I had a son.

I didn't really get a good look at the pictures. Now that I'm staring at the pictures, I can see the resemblance. I've always wanted a son so that I could play basketball with him, take him to the barbershop, and play video games with. I've missed out on nine years of his life. Just thinking about it makes me even madder at Stacy. I had been doing good staying away from heroin. This shit only made me crave for it more, but I'm bigger than that shit. Just knowing that I have a son and a baby on the way is more than enough motivation to never touch it again.

After a couple of hours, we were all out of lock up and headed home. With all the chaos going on, I didn't want Stacy to go back to the house that Juan had given her. I was glad she decided to come back to our house. The last couple of days have been rough on her. I had already added stress to her already full plate. She needed me now more than ever. The only thing that mattered right now is that she and my unborn child are cool.

"What are you doing up?" Stacy asked as she came and sat next to me on the couch.

I couldn't help but to stare at her. She still looked the same as the day I met her in the airport. She noticed the pictures of our son on the coffee table. She grabbed them and stared for a long time before she spoke up.

"He was born on Christmas Day. He weighed eight pounds, nine ounces. I took one look at him and all I could see was you. I named him after you, In case you were wondering. His adoption is not a traditional adoption. My really good friend, Vanessa, is raising him. She is considered to be his parental guardian. Legally, she has no rights to him. It was just an agreement that we made. I send money every month and we talk on the phone quite often. He knows that his real parents live in another state. I'm sorry for not telling you when we first got in contact with one another. I had no idea that we would fall back in love and get married."

As Stacy talked more and more about this friend, I started to get an uneasy feeling. My street senses were kicking in big time.

"How much can you trust the woman who has him? I find it odd that Lupe of all people knows about him. The one person you were hiding him from all of sudden pops up out the blue and informs you that she knows about your son. That shit don't sit well with me. Call her and ask to speak with him."

Stacy got up and retrieved her phone from her purse. I watched as she dialed the number. I signaled for her to put it on speakerphone. It rang for a minute and finally someone answered.

"I've been expecting your call. You have twenty-four hours to bring me the ten million or he dies just like his precious Vanessa. You need to be more careful of who you leave your children with. Money has a way of making people talk."

"Please don't hurt him, Lupe. I'll give you the money." I signaled for Stacy to keep talking. Maybe she'd give us some clues.

"I'm glad that you said that. I have someone who wants to talk to you."

After a moment of silence, a woman's voice came on the line. "Please hurry, Stacy!"

It was Ammenah. Lupe had kidnapped our son and Ammenah.

"I'll call you tomorrow with the address." Lupe hung up and Stacy just sat there in a daze.

"Don't worry Baby. We're going to get Kendrick and Ammenah back home safe and sound. I'm about to call your brothers and the rest of the family and let them know what's going on. We have to get Gail and the rest of the kids to a safe location."

I kissed Stacy on the forehead and started making calls to the family. I can't wait to off this bitch Lupe. She better not lay a finger on my son or Ammenah. Once all this shit is over, we need to take a long ass vacation. I feel like I'm in a never-ending episode of *The First 48*.

Chapter 29- Aja

I was so happy to know that Brooklyn was going to be okay. That would have killed me if she had lost her life to all of the senseless violence going on in the streets. Too many innocent babies are losing their lives. The last thing I would want is for my Lil Momma to become a statistic. Karima better hope I never catch her ass in the streets. I'm definitely going to beat the shit out of her again. I can't believe she put Brooklyn in harm's way like that. There is no telling what type of shit Marlo was doing in the streets.

Since Rahmeek refused to leave Brooklyn's side, I decided to go home and grab a couple of items. I wanted to get him a change of clothes and some personal hygiene items. Rahmeek had Brooklyn moved to a private room and it looked so plain to me. I wanted to get some of her toys and teddy bears to put a little color in her room. Rahmeek thought I was crazy, but Brooklyn needs to be around the things she loves. That will make her feel better.

"Call me as soon as you make it to the house. Go straight there. Do not make any stops."

Rahmeek was so worried about something happening to me. I had to reassure him that I would be just fine. I kissed him and Brooklyn then left the hospital. I made it to my house in less than twenty minutes. I ran inside, grabbed everything I needed, and was back out of the door within fifteen minutes. As I drove back to the hospital, I remembered that I forgot to call Rahmeek. I used my hands free device to call him. As soon as the phone started ringing, I crashed head on into another car. The impact was so strong that it caused my car to flip over several times.

"Hello! Aja!"

I could hear Rahmeek calling my name, but I was unable to speak or move. I could see everything around me and my car was flipped upside down. I observed a set of hands reach in and pull me out of the window. I was in so much pain that I couldn't move or put up a fight. The person was wearing all black. I was starting to lose consciousness. The last thing I remembered was being placed in the back of a car. Everything went black after that.

****

"Damn, you have the best pussy in the world?" I was slowly starting to come to. My vision was blurry, but I was very aware that someone was on top of me and it wasn't Rahmeek. I tried to move around but my arms were chained above my head to the headboard. I could feel the pain in between my legs as I was been raped. I was so dry it felt like I was being cut with a knife each time the person thrust in and out of me.

"Why the fuck aren't you getting wet for me?" The slap that was delivered to my face made me alert and I was able to now see the person's face.

"Marlo! Why are you doing this to me?" I was moving around trying to get him off of me.

"Shut the fuck up and don't move again. I got something that will get you wet. Remember you used to let me eat that pussy all the time. I was the first nigga to ever give you an orgasm. Now you're acting all brand new on a nigga."

Tears streamed down my face as Marlo buried his face in between my legs. He was sucking and biting on my inner thighs. I knew that there would be bite marks and bruises. He started to do the same to my pussy. He was not trying to pleasure me; he was trying to inflict pain on me. He eased his way back up to my face and tried to kiss me on the mouth. I tried to move my face but he held my bottom lip in between his teeth. He bit it until he drew blood. He inserted himself back inside of me and continued to roughly thrust inside and out of me.

"Please stop, Marlo. You don't have to do this to me!"

"I said shut the fuck up!"

He punched me so hard in the jaw I felt like he broke it. I just laid there silent as tears streamed down my face. I was blaming myself for getting myself in this predicament. He raped me for hours. I went to sleep. It was the daylight when I woke up. I looked around the room and I tried to figure out where the hell I was.

I looked on the dresser and that's when I saw a picture of Brooklyn and Rahmeek. This nigga was holding me hostage in Karima's house. I looked to the other side of the room and looked at what I appeared to be someone on the floor. I thought it was Marlo but when I focused my eyes, it was Karima's lifeless body. She was face down and blood was all over her body.

I screamed at the top of my lungs. I couldn't believe he had killed Karima. I didn't agree with her lifestyle but she didn't deserve to be killed.

"That bitch crossed me for that nigga Rahmeek just like you. I suggest you get with the program before you end up just like her. You need to get cleaned up so we can hit that nigga's safe."

Marlo unchained me and roughly yanked me up from the bed. He took me into the bathroom and pushed me over into the tub. I hit the back of my head on the wall.

"You have five minutes."

He laid a pair of jeans and a long sleeve shirt on the toilet seat. I cut the water on and I kept it running. I did a quick wash up and I started to look around for something. This motherfucker was not about to kill me. I had every intention of going home to Rahmeek, Lil Rah, and Brooklyn. He had to be out of his mind if he thought I would ever help him rob my husband. I quickly threw on the clothes he gave me. I opened of the medicine cabinet real slow so that he wouldn't hear it. I found a Twinkle razor that some people used to split hair tracks or arch eyebrows. I slid it up my arm sleeve and held on to it tight.

"Come on. I have shit to do, Aja."

He yanked the door open just as I had closed the medicine cabinet. He walked ahead of me. I knew that I had to strike if I wanted to get out of here alive. I slid the blade down into my hand. I made sure to get a good grip on the handle. As soon as he turned around to grab me, I swung the blade and it sliced him from his temple down to his chin. He was bleeding profusely and all I could see was white meat.

"I'm about to kill you, bitch!"

He pulled his gun from his waistband and pointed it at me. Gunshots rang out and Marlo's body dropped to the floor. I turned towards the door and Niyah was standing there with the smoking gun still in her hand. She was shaking so bad. I had to pry the gun out of her hand. I held her as she broke down to the floor.

"It's okay, Niyah. We have to go before the police come."

We both ran out of the house and we sped away in Niyah's car. On our way to my house, she filled me in on Ammenah and Stacy's son being held captive by Lupe. This family can't catch a break. If it ain't one thing, it's another

Chapter 30- Rahmeek

"Bro, what the fuck is going on? It must be let's fuck with Rahmeek week. First, my daughter gets shot. Next, my mother is kidnapped and now my fucking wife is missing. How the fuck do you have a car accident and simply disappear? We've been everywhere looking for her. She's not at any of the hospitals. I have a bad feeling about this. Did Niyah call back yet?"

"Calm down, Rah! The drop is tonight. We've got it all planned out. Momma gon' get out of there in one piece, trust me. Niyah is out right now trying to find Marlo to see if he knows where Aja is."

"If that nigga hurts her, I swear I'm going to jail!"

I had never in my life cried for any woman other than my grandmother. Aja had me shedding tears and balling like a baby. Regardless of my fuck ups in our relationship, I love and worship the ground she walks on. They might as well bury me if something happens to her.

"I'm so ready to kill me a motherfucker." Markese said as he leaned his head back on the couch in frustration. I know how much Markese loves Aja so I know he's going through it too.

"Damn! Ya'll sitting around acting like I died or something."

I looked up towards the door and Aja was standing there with her hands on her hips. I also noticed Niyah come in and run straight Hassan.

"I've been worried sick about you."

Markese and I both held onto her tight. I looked in her face and noticed the visible bruises on her face. I grabbed her hand and we went to our bedroom.

"What happened, Aja?"

"Marlo had kidnapped me. He took me back to Karima's house. I really don't want to tell you this, but he killed Karima. There was so much blood around her body." Aja looked down at the floor as she stumbled over her words.

"He raped me repeatedly. I'm so sorry. If I had never slept with him in the first place, this never would have happened. If Niyah would not have shown up when she did, he would have killed me."

I grabbed her and hugged her tight as she cried in my arms. "How did Niyah know he was at Karima's house?"

"She said when she got him a phone, she had put a tracking device on it just in case something happened to him. She just killed him, Rah. I feel so sorry for her."

"She'll be okay. She's surrounded by all of us. We'll help her deal with it."

God has come through for a nigga again in a matter of forty-eight hours. My daughter was going to pull through and my wife was back home where she belonged. Now all I needed to do was get my mother back in one piece.

"I need you to get you some clothes and go downtown to the Palmer House. That's where Gail, the kids, and the rest of the girls are. Nisa and KJ have been moved to a private hospital. I sent Brooklyn with her. We have to move everybody to a safe location while we go and get Ammenah and Stacy's son back. Stacy has to stay behind with us because she has to make the drop."

"I love you so much, Rah."

"I love you too, Aja."

We both stood there and held onto one another until I finally broke our embrace. Aja packed some clothes and I had a driver take her and

Niyah downtown to the hotel. Once I made it back to the crib, we sat around and went over the plans. The address that Lupe had given Stacy was Juan's old address. No one had lived in that house since Carmen killed him. Stacy would be going in by herself but we would be in the vicinity. There's a wooded area that surrounds the house where we would be stationed. After packing the money up the way Lupe requested, we were on our way to make the drop. Unbeknownst to her, she would never see a dime of the money.

As we lay in the bushes, we found our targets. As soon as the security guards saw the red beams flashing in their faces, it was too late. They were already dead. Once we had killed all the security, we were ready to move inside of the house. We watched the perimeter of the house to make sure no one tried to leave or enter. Everything was going as planned until I saw four figures creeping around in the backyard trying to get inside.

"Do ya'll see what I'm seeing? Those figures look mighty familiar." I asked Markese, Boogie, Killa, and Hassan.

"Those are the beasts that ya'll created. Now let's get in here before they get us all killed," Boogie said as we made our towards the estate

Chapter 31- Stacy

I was nervous as hell standing on the porch of this run down ass estate. I rang the doorbell for what seemed like forever before Chico opened the door. He looked around before he pulled me into the house. As he escorted me back to an office, he made sure to cop a free feel on my ass. I walked into the office and Lupe was sitting behind the desk.

"I'm glad you're following instructions."

She tried to reach for the bag of money, but I quickly yanked it away."Where is my son and my mother? I need to see them before I hand over the money."

"I'm running this fucking show. Hand over the money now!"

Lupe stood up and pointed her gun at me. Out of nowhere, the bookcase turned around and out walked Nisa, Trish, Niyah, and Aja.

"Actually, we're running this show." Nisa said as she had her gun aimed at Lupe and she threw one to me.

"Where the fuck did you cunts come from?" As the words left Chico's his mouth, I shot him in between the eyes. He went down instantly.

"Can we kill this bitch now?" Trish said as she stepped closer to Lupe pressing the gun into her forehead. "You have that same look as Carmen did before I burned her ass alive."

Lupe tried to grab Trish but she wasn't quick enough. Trish brought the gun down on the bridge of her nose and broke it instantly.

"Where the fuck is my mother and son, you crazy bitch?" I gave her ass a leg shot because I was tired of her stalling.

Lupe fell to the floor in pain. "They're in the attic," she managed to say. Niyah and Aja ran out of the room and went to find the attic.

"I have to ask you, Lupe, why did you do this? You have more money than you know what to do with. Why would you want ten million dollars from me?"

"It wasn't about the money. It was about making you and your whore of a mother suffer for ruining my life. Your existence has taken away all hopes of me having the American Dream that I was supposed to have."

This woman had forgotten how much pain she had caused not only me but also my brothers and my mother. We missed out on a lifetime together. I raised my gun and ended it all for her ass. It was only right that now I can move on with my life without looking over my shoulder. I stood over her, still pointing the gun at her after I emptied my clip in her.

"It's over, baby." Boogie said as he took the gun from my hands.

"Look, who I found." Boogie held our son's hand and we all stood there hugging. I placed kisses all over his face.

"They didn't hurt you, did they?" he shook his head no and wrapped his arms around my waist. I looked up and I saw everybody hugging and kissing one another.

"Let's go home, Ma. It's been a long week." Boogie kissed me passionately and we walked out hand in hand with our son.

Epilogue

The sun shined brightly as the high waves of water splashed against the rocks on the beach. The sound of R.Kelly singing his song *Just Like That* in the background fit perfectly for the occasion. All of the couples danced with one another as they celebrated their three-year wedding anniversary. The whole family was in Punta Cana, Mexico celebrating another year of being together. All of the trials and tribulations were worth it as they all danced and looked into each other's eyes. There wasn't a place in the world that they would rather be at this moment. Everyone was dressed in all white and a hint of turquoise.

Aja couldn't help but to smile as she rubbed her hands on the back of Rahmeek's head. He had cut all his dreads off. She thought that he was even more handsome as she admired his fresh haircut. Aja couldn't help but to think back to the first time she had ever laid eyes on him. There were plenty of bitches in the strip club that night, but he only had eyes for her. She glanced over his shoulder and watched as Brooklyn and Lil Rah played in the sand. She loved her family and they made her complete. At that moment, the cheating and the lies that almost brought them down didn't even matter. They were together and happy. That was the only thing that mattered to her.

Rahmeek looked into Aja's eyes and knew that he was a lucky motherfucker. He regretted all of the bullshit that he had put her through. Aja was the love of his life and he wouldn't trade her for nothing in the world. He laughed inwardly as he thought about how he had murked two nigga's over her. Aja belonged to him and him only.

This girl gon' be the death of me, he thought to himself as he rubbed her protruding belly. She was now five months pregnant with their second son. There wasn't a doubt in his mind that they would grow old together.

He couldn't see himself being with anyone else. God had created Aja especially for him.

Markese and Trish were hugging each other so tight as they slow danced. Markese knew that she was too good of a woman to have stayed with him. He hated himself for all the times he physically abused her. In reality, he was mad about his own fuck-ups and he took it out on her. He knew that he had put Trish through hell. Every day he thanked God for her staying with him. He knew that she had every reason to leave and never look back. He laughed as he thought about her holding his ass at gunpoint. These days he treads real lightly in her presence. Trish was still in beast mode and on his ass like a hawk. He placed a soft kiss on her lips and she laid her head on his shoulder.

Trish's mind drifted back to the day Markese had taken her virginity. Everything was simple back then when they didn't have money. All they had was one another and that was enough. It still hurt her when she first saw Carmen and Markese walking with Gabriella and Juan. She wiped a tear that started to form. Her crying days were over.

Carmen was no longer in control. She was in hell where she belonged. She showed Markese her inner strength that had been hidden for so long. Looking at Gabriella, Juan and Lil Markese she knew that they all deserved a happily ever after. Without a doubt in her mind she knew that Markese loved her and she loved him. Their love could conquer anything. Standing there with one another was living proof of it. The police had been looking at Markese and Trish as the prime suspect in Carmen's murder. After a lengthy investigation the case was closed due to lack of evidence. They were happy that they could finally move on with their life.

Niyah held onto Hassan as if the world was about to come to an end. She hated that she let Marlo come in and wreak havoc on her marriage.

Prior to his arrival, they never had issues in their marriage. She wanted Hassan to know that she appreciated him and everything that he did for her. All she had was him and the twins. Her mother severed all ties with her after hearing of Marlo's death. She felt like Niyah didn't protect him enough. Her mother was not aware that Niyah had killed Marlo. Niyah had nightmares on a regular basis. Hassan was right there to hold her until she fell back to sleep. Hassan was her knight in shining armor and her heart belonged to him. Hassan Jr. and Hadiyah ran over to their parents and began to dance with them. Hassan pulled his family into his embrace and knew that life without them would be nothing. Niyah was the love of his life and she made life worth living.

Nisa laughed as she tried dancing with Killa. He had no damn rhythm. She was so happy that he finally forgave her for getting an abortion. The birth of their son brought them closer together. He beat the odds despite the fact that they were stacked against him. Nisa and Killa had to rely on each other for the strength to make it through their newest battle.

Remi had left her baby on their doorstep. After a DNA test confirmed Killa as the father, Nisa was now raising both kids as her own. Not one time did she complain or curse about it. Killa was her husband and she was going to support him no matter what. Killa placed soft kisses on her neck. He couldn't help but think about how Nisa went from being a stone cold killer to the perfect wife and mother. That's all he ever wanted was for Nisa to be his wife. They would always hold court in the streets if they needed to, but her wife and motherly duties came first. Nisa had no arguments with that. She loved being a mother and a wife. All she ever wanted was Killa's love and affection. She had that and so much more.

Boogie looked in Stacy's eyes and mouthed *I love you* as they slow danced. Boogie never knew what love was until Stacy came into his life.

Stacy showed him the true meaning of love each and every day. Many times, he would find himself staring at his son Kendrick Jr. and his newborn daughter Madison. He could never hurt them or bring any harm to them, the way that his parents had did him. Stacy had given him the greatest gift a woman could give a man that had no family. A family of his own.

Stacy mouthed *I love you too* as she glanced over at Kendrick Jr. holding his little sister and feeding her. She was so happy that Boogie forgave her. She loved Boogie with all her heart and she couldn't see herself being with any other man. Her life had come full circle. She had a family of her own. Not to mention two brothers and mother that she never knew she had. God had worked things out in her favor. He knew she had nothing and no one. It was meant for her to be in the airport at the same time as Boogie when they first met.

After finding all those bricks, the guys jumped back into the drug game like they never left. Behind the scenes of course. They're still running their businesses on a daily basis. One would look at them walking around in their business attire and never know that they were flooding the streets with the best heroin the city of Chicago had ever seen. The crew finally had the street status that they all had worked so hard far. It wasn't easy getting but it was worth the fight. The couples did what they had to do as a family and they came out on top. From the very beginning, there was always a question of loyalty amongst them. They all proved that their loyalty was with each other. They had LOVE for one another, the LOYALTY to one another, and the RESPECT they earned from the streets.

THE END

Acknowledgements

First and foremost giving all praises to God Almighty. It's your will that has brought me this far.

To the loves of my life, Larry and Latrell, please forgive me for the countless days I spend in my room writing or on the computer. Everything I do I am doing to make a better life for you guys. All of my hard work will pay off for all of us in the future. I love the both of you with all my heart.

To my parents, siblings, nieces, nephews, cousins and my entire family I love you all and thank you for all your support.

A very special thanks to Myss Shan for not only being my publisher, but also a really great confidant and friend. I am so thankful for you. I want to be the first to let you know that your hard work does not go unnoticed. You believed in me from the start and I am forever grateful for you

A very special thanks to Jackie Chanel. It was an honor to be a part of the Black Starr Productions Family.

To my readers I am so thankful for each and every one of you. Thank you for all of your support.

Last but not least, To David Weaver and the entire Team Bankroll Squad Family I am so happy to be a part of such a great movement. It's an honor to be surrounded by so much talent. #SALUTE

I would like to dedicate this book to Ronald Deshawn Hayes Jr. who left this Earth way too soon. You're forever in our hearts and you're truly missed. Continue to watch over your mother and your siblings.

Connect with Mz. Lady P!!

Facebook: Mzladyp Theauthor

Instagram: Mzladyp819

Copyright Notice

Living for Love, Dying for Loyalty 3
Copyright 2014 by Mz. Lady P
Published by Black Starr Productions
All Rights Reserved

Table of Contents

Main Menu

Chapter 1-Rahmeek

Chapter 2- Stacy

Chapter 3- Boogie

Chapter 4-Niyah

Chapter 5- Aja

Chapter 6- Rahmeek

Chapter 7- Trish

Chapter 8-Carmen

Chapter 9- Markese

Chapter 10- Nisa

Chapter 11- Killa

Chapter 12- Carmen

Chapter 13 -Markese

Chapter 14-Trish

Chapter 15- Momma Gail

Chapter 16-Aja

Chapter 17- Rahmeek

Chapter 18- Hassan

Chapter 19-Niyah

Chapter 20-Marlo

Chapter 21- Nisa

Chapter 22-Trish

Chapter 23- Markese

Chapter 24-Lupe Rodriquez

Chapter 25- Stacy

Chapter 26- Rahmeek

Chapter 27-Karima

Chapter 28-Boogie

Chapter 29- Aja

Chapter 30- Rahmeek

Chapter 31- Stacy

Epilogue

Acknowledgements

Copyright Notice

CPSIA information can be obtained
at www.ICGtesting.com
Printed in the USA
LVOW10s1319270318
571320LV00019B/539/P

9 781505 586602